HOW
IT
HAPPENED
IN
PEACH
HILL

HOW
IT
HAPPENED
IN
PEACH
HILL

marthe jocelyn

LAUREL-LEAF BOOKS

Copyright © 2007 by Marthe Jocelyn

All rights reserved. Published by Laurel-Leaf, an imprint of Random House Children's Books, a division of Random House, Inc., New York. Originally published in hardcover by Wendy Lamb Books, an imprint of Random House Children's Books, New York, in 2007.

Laurel-Leaf and the colophon are registered trademarks of Random House, Inc.

Visit us on the Web! www.randomhouse.com/teens

Educators and librarians, for a variety of teaching tools, visit us at
www.randomhouse.com/teachers

The Library of Congress has cataloged the hardcover edition of this work as follows:
Jocelyn, Marthe.
How it happened in Peach Hill / Marthe Jocelyn.
p. cm.
Summary: When fifteen-year-old Annie Grey and her "clairvoyant" mother arrive in Peach Hill, New York, in 1924, each finds a reason for wanting to finally settle down, but to reach their goals they will have to do some serious lying and Annie will have to stand up for herself.
ISBN: 978-0-375-83701-2 (trade) — ISBN: 978-0-375-93701-9 (glb)
ISBN: 978-0-375-89285-1 (e-book)
[1. Mothers and daughters—Fiction. 2. Swindlers and swindling—Fiction.
3. Self-realization—Fiction. 4. Clairvoyance—Fiction.
5. New York (State)—History—20th century—Fiction.] I. Title.
PZ7.J579How 2007
[Fic]—dc22
2006026688

ISBN: 978-0-375-83702-9 (pbk.)

RL: 5.6
Printed in the United States of America
10 9 8 7 6 5 4 3 2 1

First Laurel-Leaf Edition

For Jerry, AJ and Pa
And all the beloved spirits on the Other Side

1

**Put salt on the
doorstep of a new house
and no evil can enter.**

Mama taught me to lie.

Some would say that Mama went to jail in Carling, New York, because of lies, but we had other ideas.

We knew that the truth came in different varieties and that most people had a favorite. Same thing with untruth. Anyone could decide what to call a lie, so sometimes there'd be a misunderstanding.

Mama made claims to being clairvoyant: able to "see clearly" what was unseen by everyone else. She had what she called a sensitive way with the spirit world. I was her assistant. We offered services that only we could perform. Mama cultivated her talents to help people seeking solace, or relief from a predicament.

When a gentleman, for instance, misplaced a gold watch and offered a reward for its recovery, Mama's psychic ability was almost certain to detect the missing object. Particularly when her beguiling smile and her nimble fingers had caused the misplacement to begin with, and I had selected the discovery site. When the gentleman reclaimed his property, we were handsomely paid, and everyone was content.

Until an incident of faulty timing led to a watch being observed in our possession.

That day in Carling, I was fifteen. I watched Mama being dragged away by the police with her stockings torn and her feet scrabbling to touch the ground. I saw her hat flung to the pavement, with the ostrich feather snapped under a boot. I wanted to howl and kick somebody. That sickening scene played over and over in front of my eyes, like at the moving pictures with the pianist gone home.

And while Mama languished for two days and nights in the stone cellar of that Carling police station behind a wall of iron mesh, I was confined to the sheriff's home. The sheriff's wife was a more formidable jailer than any of the young men with pistols who were watching over Mama.

"We've had villains in here before, Miss Annie Grey." She jabbed her finger at me. "But never one so young, nor so unrepentant!"

Well, what was I supposed to be repenting for? We didn't want the watch, we wanted the money for its recovery, and we never got that, so how could we repent?

"You sit right there and read aloud from the Good Book. Your mother has some nerve, with her claims to see into the future. No one but the good Lord can say what awaits us! I know what awaits *you*, young lady. You will read, without moving, from the moment you finish your breakfast until I put your supper on the table tonight. . . ."

At first I didn't think it was much of a punishment. There are some great moments of drama in the Bible, storms and miracles, plenty of evil doings and heroic characters.

" 'And God divided the Light from Darkness!' " I thundered, waving my fist in the air, " 'and God called the light Day and He called the dark Night. . . .' "

But the sheriff's wife didn't want my interpretation. She wanted my piety and she wanted it plain.

"Don't you get fanciful and don't you rest."

I had no wish to repeat that experience as long as I lived. I chose to have an epileptic seizure at the same moment that Mama agreed to marry her guard, and so between us we negotiated our freedom.

Luckily, Mama prided herself on always being prepared for trouble. Our savings were neatly arranged in the false bottom of our trunk and hadn't been disturbed by the rude officers who had searched our belongings. We left town the very hour Mama was released, and we swore not to repeat our errors. Mama said soon we would have enough money to buy a home of our own. She said we could settle down, just as I'd been begging for, so long as I could remember.

We arrived in Hawley feeling breathless, as if we'd run all the way from Carling in our fine leather Hi-Cuts, instead of sitting in a first-class compartment with a Thermos of chamomile tea and a two-pound box of coconut macaroons. We stayed in Hawley just long enough to come up with a new twist to our old game.

"One of our strengths is your sweet and innocent face," said Mama. "We'll take it one step further and turn you into a dim-witted angel. You will be clucked over and then ignored by heartless women who think only of themselves. This will put you in an excellent position for eavesdropping."

Mama was sharp; no mistake about that. She was a fake as far as hearing from the dead, or even seeing the outcome of a situation ahead of time, but she had a sensitive way about her, when required professionally. She was a master at drawing out secrets. With a little background information, she easily appeared to see straight into the hearts of forlorn and desperate seekers—usually women—who spent heaps of money to hear the advice of a stranger. And Mama was so pretty, people tended to trust her without thinking about it.

So, in Hawley, I sat for hours holding Mama's mirror with the tortoiseshell handle. I perfected the ability to cross one eye while my mouth stayed open. I breathed out with a faint wheeze so that my lips dried up or even crusted. Once in a while I'd add a twitch.

If anyone had looked through the window, they would have heard Mama scolding me, "Get rid of that smart glint in your eyes. And let your lips gape!"

"It makes me thirsty, having my tongue lolling out."

"Try honking through your nose when you laugh. That will give your mouth a rest."

I experimented on the streets of Hawley. People would take a first look at me and shiver with disgust. They'd look again and think, Oh, the poor thing, thank the heavens she's not mine. And then they'd ignore me, just as Mama had predicted, out of politeness, maybe, or embarrassment.

That was the moment I could go to work.

While in disguise I planned to gather gossip and bring it

home to Mama. She would put it to use in little ways, giving it back to the very same people, only shaped differently and in exchange for money. Lots of money, over time.

We moved on to Peach Hill toward the end of summer, to start fresh. The days were still hot and I wished we could go closer to the shores of the Finger Lakes, but Mama said resort towns attracted more sophisticated people. We were better off in Nowhere, New York.

There was not a peach tree in sight. There was a hill, though, dotted with fancy houses that might have had peach trees before they had swimming pools and rose gardens. Below the hill, it was an ordinary town like all the others we'd ever stayed in; big enough for a train station, a church, and a cinema, but small enough to see most of it during an evening stroll. The edge of town wasn't an edge so much as a fading away, with a few more tumbledown houses before the farms and fields began in earnest.

I felt shivers that first night, in spite of it being August. It was pretty here, and I wondered if this would be the place where our savings would add up high enough to find a nest. We'd abandoned most of our possessions in Carling, so we had only the trunk and a few bundles to carry from the taxicab into our new, furnished rooms at 62 Needle Street.

"Look there," Mama whispered. "The curtain is quivering at number fifty-nine across the road."

I slid my tongue out and let my eye droop.

"Put up the sign before you heat the kettle, Annie," said Mama. "We'll have customers by nightfall tomorrow."

It never took long for word of our arrival to flutter around a town like a flock of birds. People might scorn us in public, but nearly everyone had a reason to seek us out on the quiet. Our rooms were on the ground floor, just off the main square, where people could find us easily. It wasn't showy; we didn't want anyone feeling nervous. But we gussied it up enough to suggest that our talents were worth the investment.

We took care setting up the front room, where Mama received company. We were lucky that the rooms provided a red cut-velvet armchair for the customer and a smaller, wooden one for Mama. We hired a polished table to place in between, one that could be enlarged, as needed, when we were hosting what Mama referred to as a calling. We could seat eight as the occasion demanded. By day, an ivory lace curtain dappled the light, almost like in a chapel. The sign in the window, lettered in gold script, announced MADAME CATERINA, SPIRITUAL ADVISOR.

Mama's circulars claimed that we had Gypsy blood, but our tawny skin and black hair were really thanks to her grandmother, a Mexican maid in her grandfather's house. Saying "Gypsy" meant more to the customers, that was all, making them think that wanderlust and fortune-telling came naturally.

Peach Hill was our eighth town, Mama's and mine, if you didn't calculate the hundreds of places we'd stayed three nights each while we worked with Lenny's Famous Fun Fair. We joined Lenny when I was maybe four or five. When I was about nine, the United States joined the Great War and people had better things to do with their money than spend it on fun. Lenny closed up shop and we were forced to make our own fortune.

We moved a few times in the beginning, but for most of the war we lived in Deacon, where the factory made buttons for uniforms. That place was filled with sad, lonely wives, working on the assembly line and praying that their gleaming buttons would not be blown off the chests of distant husbands.

It was in Deacon where we first began to prosper. All those funerals were not just because of the war, but also because of the great influenza epidemic. There was likely not a family in town, or anywhere else, who did not release a soul or two through that deadly illness. But it was mainly the young men gone to be soldiers who brought us the clientele.

"I beg you! I beg you, on my knees!" a lady would say as soon as I opened the door. "Read my palm, look at the cards, pour out the tea leaves, whatever it takes, just tell me that my Davey (or my Joe, my Marco, my Terence) is still alive. . . ."

Not hearing from overseas for weeks or months could drive a woman crazy. Mama had to be careful about her wording on those occasions, wanting a return visit whatever the outcome.

"Ooh," she'd murmur. "I'm seeing a place of great darkness and confusion. Your loved one needs you to be strong and patient. . . ."

When bad news came, it was no surprise that people hurried back to our parlor. The war had a positive outcome for Mama and me, aside from stomping out the wicked tyrants overseas who threatened peace and liberty. It left thousands of mothers and sweethearts and wives aching to connect with their lost boys now dwelling on the Other Side.

Mama plied her trade, and we learned an important lesson: Heartbreak is very good for business.

7

2

A young lady should never sing while cooking; she will marry an aged man.

The first true test of my new character was Peg, hired on to keep house for us. Peg was maybe twenty-five, taller than Mama, with strong arms and a long nose, and curly hair bouncing off her head. Peg liked to sing while she worked and didn't mind that our busiest day was Saturday.

"My daddy doesn't want me to have a beau," she admitted. "Saturdays last forever without a dance to think about."

At first I thought Peg was as slow as I pretended to be, the way she shook her head from side to side while Mama gave instructions. Then I realized she just couldn't believe what she was hearing. Mama tossed in extras so that Peg would have something to gossip about in town.

"Turn the pillowcases inside out on the beds, Peg. Makes the spirits restless and readier to communicate."

"Yes'm."

"And never lean the broom against a bed, or the person who sleeps there will soon die."

"Yes'm. I mean, No, ma'am."

"And Peg?"

"Yes'm?"

"Call me 'madame,' Peg. Not 'yes'm.' I'm a clairvoyant, not a butcher's wife."

"Yes'm."

"If someone knocks, Peg, tell her I'm with a client and make an appointment for the next day."

"But ma'am, that would be a fib."

"My clients are not all among the living, Peg. To receive news from the Other Side, I must keep in contact with the spirits every day."

"Oh," said Peg.

"Precisely," said Mama. "So it is not a fib to tell people at the door that I am otherwise engaged, even if you cannot see my customer."

"Yes'm."

We soon had the opportunity to test the system. A day or two later, Peg answered a knock while Mama and I were tidying the front room.

"Madame is engaged with the dead," we heard her say. "If you come tomorrow, Mrs. Romero, she can see you at eleven o'clock."

"Well done, Peg," said Mama, sending her off with a smile before turning to me. "Annie, you heard the name. Why are you dawdling? Go."

I hurried to the window and caught a glimpse of a green jacket as Mrs. Romero rounded the corner. I snatched my hat and my notebook and slipped out the door to follow her.

It wasn't my first time out. I'd practiced in Hawley and I'd already circled Peach Hill a few times, observing where women gathered and gossip flowed. I'd pinpointed the best places for eavesdropping: the benches in the square, the front table in Bing's Café, and wandering around Carlaw's, the greengrocer's. Women seemed to loiter there long beyond buying potatoes and peas. I wrote in a code I'd made up, so no one else could decipher it. After each excursion, I unscrambled my code and catalogued whatever I'd heard, no matter if they were clients yet or not.

Jane Ford:
- **husband likes fried eggs sprinkled with brown sugar**
- **both parents crossed over, died of influenza**
- **favorite phrase: "Whatever next!"**

Mrs. Burly:
- **son stutters**
- **owes at the bank but has a teapot full of silver dollars**
- **poodle crossed over, hit by a motorcar**

The smallest details make the biggest impact in the darkened room of a fortune-teller.

But when I followed Mrs. Romero, it was the first time I'd plunged into the heart of the town with an active mission. I let my tongue flop out between my lips, I shuddered, and I hobbled onto Main Street. What did it matter how I behaved? I didn't know anyone here and we probably wouldn't be staying long enough to change that.

On a Thursday after lunch, I guessed that shopping for supper would be Mrs. Romero's quest. Sure enough, inside Carlaw's, I saw the green jacket next to an ivory-colored sweater. I crept closer and kept my head down. The two ladies stood over the bins of onions and potatoes. I raised one melon after another to my nose, smelling each for ripeness and listening as hard as I could.

"—just don't know what to do," Mrs. Romero was saying. "My Rosie is the biggest flirt I ever saw and going straight to hell if she keeps it up. That Joe Mackie had his hands all over her out on the porch last night!"

The other woman's voice was softer, harder to hear.

"No surprise . . . pretty face . . . full figure . . ."

"Full figure? Jane, she's got breasts the size of cabbages, make no mistake! She takes after my Frank's mother, God rest her soul, who had her underthings specially constructed in Boston."

A clerk appeared, to weigh Mrs. Romero's potatoes. The ladies hadn't seen me. I put down the melon and went outside to scribble some notes. My little notebook had a slim gold pen attached in a snug leather loop. I'd hammered a hole through the spine and hung the book around my neck on a length of blue ribbon.

When the ladies came out, I leered up at them, jiggling my eyeball as best I could.

"Well, whatever next?" The cream-sweatered lady was Jane Ford, already in my file. "I heard there was an idiot come to town. She belongs to the new fortune-teller on Needle Street."

"Poor witless thing," said Mrs. Romero.

"All the troubles in the world can't match that, eh, Aggie?"

"One look at this child and I'm happy to have my Rosie," said Mrs. Romero. "Hussy or not."

People will say anything in front of an idiot.

I watched through the window while the butcher wrapped sausages for Mrs. Romero. She came out of the cobbler's carrying a brown paper package and went into the post office. She came out of the post office chatting with a woman who wore a burgundy hat. On the open street, I couldn't hear anything more.

I followed Mrs. Romero all the way to her home on Daly Avenue. One glance at the porch showed a pair of blue-painted rockers flanking a big pot of crimson geraniums. I passed by only once, noting the chintz curtains and the Model T in the driveway. I had plenty for Mama now.

I wandered back to the square and found a place to sit near the statue of a soldier on a horse, as close as I dared to a group of kids my age. I knew it would take time, but I intended to learn the name of every child I encountered in Peach Hill. I was watching for who liked whom, who was mean, and who might be my friend if I weren't my mama's partner.

The prettiest girls were Sally Carlaw, from the greengrocer's family, and Delia, the policeman's daughter, who didn't have a mother. Those two were the honey that drew the bees. They had a gang of boys with shadowed upper lips and froggy voices who buzzed around them, showing off: Howie; Frankie Romero, who I guessed was our new client's son; and somebody called Pitts. The not-as-pretty girls seemed to have more fun than the popular ones, making up songs and practicing the shimmy or the Charleston right there in the square. There were younger kids too, eating candy or kicking a ball around.

Oh, and one odd person lurking behind the statue. A girl, but wearing boy's overalls. She was not exactly hiding, but not joining in, either. I could read the signs; she was spying, like me. She saw me looking and turned her back.

"Hey, Sammy! Sammy Sloane!"

"Sammy's home!"

A boy I hadn't seen before strolled into the park and leaned against a tree. I might as well say it; he was the most wonderful boy I ever saw. He didn't wear a cap like the others. His black hair flopped and blew around his handsome face like, well, like shiny black hair. I quickly learned that he'd been away at his uncle's farm for the summer and come back in time for the new school term.

I forgot myself and stared with both eyes, admiring his face, his shoulders, his laughing voice. Someone sat on the other end of my bench. It was the peculiar girl, inspecting me.

"Ha," she said. "What's your game?"

I jerked my eyeball into motion and produced a tremor so severe that I fell off the bench by accident. I jumped to my feet with hot cheeks. The girl was gone in a flash, but the rest of them were looking at me.

"Hey, Teddy!" called the older boy named Howie. "See the idiot over there?"

I froze. I heard a ripple of choked-back laughter.

"Uh-huh," said the little one named Teddy. He was in overalls, his hair bristling like hay.

"I dare you to touch her. That's all you gotta do. Touch her and run for your life."

"What do I get?" said Teddy.

Even in my agitation, I had to admire his practicality.

13

"You get to tell us if she's got skin like a lizard," said Howie.

"No, thanks," said Teddy.

"I'll give you a penny." Delia stood up and opened a pink coin purse. "I double dare you. She's the ugliest thing I ever saw and you'd be a brave big fella to go anywhere near." She held out a coin to the little boy, who now was tempted, I could see.

I felt sick and sweaty all over. My eye was tired and my tongue was dry. I backed away as Teddy tiptoed forward.

"Aw, leave her alone. What's she done to bother you?" It was my new hero, Sammy Sloane, but too late. Teddy darted forward with his fingers outstretched. I turned and ran, pursued by hooting and jeers.

"Hey! Moron!"

I felt a sharp bite on the back of my arm and then another on my neck.

"Got her! Did you see that?"

"Good shot, Frankie! Like hitting a giant squirrel!"

They were throwing stones at me! I clapped my hand to the stinging spot above my collar and felt a sticky dribble of blood. I kept running, jagged sobs escaping like steam from a locomotive.

Peg found me crying in the kitchen.

"I'm ugly! I'm so ugly!"

"Ah, now," said Peg. "There, there." She washed the scratches and patted my back till I settled down. I might have been her baby sister.

"Peg loves Annie," she began, slowly as always when

14

talking to me. "Peg knows better than the lunks in the square. You'd be quite pretty if you wore a cute hat that shaded your eyes, never mind there's a vacancy between your ears. Not quite so pretty as your mama, but near enough. Try closing your mouth, if you can. And wash your hair once in a while, for pity's sake!"

She had me lean over the side of the sink while she gave my head a scrubbing. Is this what normal mothers do? I wondered. She doused my hair with freshly squeezed lemon juice before the final rinse.

"Annie loves Peg," I said, playing my part.

Alone in my room later, I panicked. What if pretending to be stupid and clumsy was turning me stupid and clumsy? I made myself recite poems backward and the date of every battle during the Civil War. I practiced juggling, using two shoes and a hairbrush.

I sat with the mirror in my hand, twisting my face into idiotic grimaces and then just staring at my own reflection. Was I pretty at all? Could a boy ever look at me and think so? Could Sammy Sloane?

In the morning, I crawled into my corner while Mama was fixing her hair. She didn't like me nearby when she was working, but I'd found a way around that. I'd inched the big chair in the front room into such a position that I could sit behind it with my knees scrunched up and my back in the crook of the wall.

Mrs. Romero arrived promptly at eleven o'clock. Mama sat her down and held her hands for a moment. "I could read your palm, Mrs. Romero," Mama began. "But the vibrations from the spirit world are very strong this morning. There's an older woman here from the Other Side, with a message for you. She has a matronly bosom and says she's family but not related by blood."

Mrs. Romero gasped. "Mother Romero? Frank's mother? She died of the influenza five years ago, May 1919."

"She's worried about your daughter," said Mama. "Your daughter who is named for a flower."

"That's Rose," said Mrs. Romero.

"But I'm seeing another flower too," said Mama. "Bright red, like passion."

"I don't know. Rose is my only girl."

"It could be a real flower," prompted Mama.

"Oh," said Mrs. Romero. "We have geraniums on the porch."

"That's likely it. The porch . . . and passion . . ." Mama's voice trailed off, letting the words simmer.

"I don't like to think of Mother Romero watching that!"

"She is suggesting that you and your husband sit out on the porch in the evenings, in the blue rockers. Rose won't be able to entertain her young man there, in the dark."

Mrs. Romero was speechless.

"You have another child," said Mama. "A boy. Is he named for his father?"

"How did you know that? Young Frankie."

"His grandmother has a message for him, too," said Mama. "She wants him to be a nice boy. No more rough language. No more slinging stones."

Mrs. Romero sighed. "I tell him again and again. He doesn't listen to me."

16

"Stop feeding him fatty meats," said Mama. "No more sausages. A tough boy needs cauliflower and Brussels sprouts to make him more sensitive."

That part was my idea. I only wished I could have watched him at supper that night.

3

The spouse who goes to sleep first on the wedding day will be the first to die.

Nearly all our customers were female, as I said. We'd get the odd young man on a matter of romance, and one fellow, Bobby Pike, who begged Mama to help him bet on the horses. But when Mr. Poole arrived, in the middle of September, along with golden light in the late afternoons, we knew the season was changing in more ways than one.

Mama had not insisted on a telephone when inquiring about rooms, as we'd not lived with one before. The fact that most people used party lines in these little towns made Mama more uneasy about sharing the service, never knowing who might be listening in. But here it was, already installed, and now *Brrrp brrrp*, crying for attention in the hallway.

Women, their first visit, often tapped on the door on an impulse, courage up. Men tended to arrange things ahead of time. Mr. Poole, a businessman, called us on the telephone to reserve an appointment for two days later.

Mama reported the conversation in full. "He is acquainted with that Mrs. Foster, who conveniently discovered she was pregnant directly after I said there was a baby in her future," Mama told me. "He asked 'What remuneration will you require?' instead of 'How much does it cost?' I think you should visit his house this evening, Annie."

It was best to view the homes of our swankier patrons after dark, when I would not be disturbing anyone inside. Mama liked to hear architectural details.

Mr. Poole lived halfway up the hill in a house with a pagoda and a lily pond, all wrapped around with a wrought iron fence. I didn't often climb fences. Although I preferred to peek through windows from an up-close position, a fence could mean a vicious dog. I chose just to stroll by as the night grew darker. Columns flanked the mansion's front door; there were marble steps and panes of stained glass set into the upstairs dormer windows. All these fine touches ensured that Mama would be most solicitous of poor, bereaved Mr. Poole.

Waiting for Peg to make supper, Mama and I reread the few notes I had about the Pooles. Mrs. Poole had died a year before, from an ailment that had her looking like a skeleton long before she passed. I knew this the same way I knew everything, from listening. She seemed to have been quite a sourpuss, who spat out insults as rapidly as an auctioneer. The ladies at the market did not get hushed or teary when her name came up.

"He never would have married her if she hadn't been so rich!" was the general sentiment. One knobbly-nosed woman had even suggested that Mr. Poole could be forgiven if he'd hurried his wife's death along with the judicious use of arsenic, but here the other ladies would not venture.

Mr. Poole:
Favors coconut hair oil.
Mrs. Poole:
Elbows sharp as carpet needles,
tongue sharper still.

Mostly there was talk of how her father must be spinning under his fancy pink granite tombstone, knowing that his estate and the inheritance from the Lovely Legs stocking factory ended up in the hands of his son-in-law.

"So much money they use five-dollar bills for kindling."

"This is a big fish, Annie," said Mama. "This demands our particular consideration."

"Do we do something different?"

"Notice details," she said, as if that weren't already my specialty.

Mr. Poole arrived on a Wednesday afternoon, nearly in disguise. Peg reported later that he wore an overcoat with the collar turned up and a hat with the brim tipped down. He knocked twice and then knocked again four seconds later before Peg even had her apron off. Mama thought I was reading in my room, but I was already settled behind the red chair. Thanks to my ingenuity and small frame, I knew from the start how things really stood with Mr. Poole.

Mr. Poole began to speak without sitting down, as if Mama were an angel descended from Heaven and would disappear before he'd got his worries off his chest. He was certain his dead wife had returned to haunt him. She didn't like the new crockery he'd chosen and she'd broken four teacups, jumping them out of his hands to the floor. She didn't approve of his introducing new fish into the pond, so she'd left two of them gasping on the bank. Mr. Poole wanted Mama to contact his dead wife and tell her to stop.

"You remind her that I'm alive and she's not," he said. "I've been drinking out of teacups covered in primroses for twenty-two years and it's time for a change."

He was pretty ruffled. Mama tucked him into the big chair I was squeezed behind and said she could see how reaching Mrs. Poole was of the utmost importance. She leaned in so close to him that I dared not breathe. She had decided to enchant while my legs got cramps, pressing up so tightly against my chest.

"Normally, Mr. Poole, I would have a calling here in this room to send the word to your late wife. But this sounds like an extreme situation." Her voice was tender, urgent, making me squirm. "I believe I will be most effective if I come to your home."

My goodness, I thought. His watch chain must be solid gold! Or he was flashing emerald cuff links and alligator shoes. It was too risky to peek.

"The spirits are often caught off guard when approached on their own territory," Mama told him. "I can likely reach her without too much difficulty."

"I see," said Mr. Poole, sounding nervous.

"I expect your wife will insist on a little coaxing to move along quietly," said Mama, making it seem she took his plight seriously. "It may not happen all in one night. But we're most likely to succeed by using elements from her earthly home; some jewelry, perhaps, and a cup of dirt from your garden. Oh, and we'll need a small advance to pay for other particular materials. I'll bring my daughter as an assistant."

"You have a daughter?" He sounded surprised—also, disappointed, perhaps.

"You may have seen her around town," said Mama. "She is an unusual child, and sadly touched in the head. It has been a struggle, being a lone widow caring for a needy child. But I have discovered that inhabitants of the Other Side are particularly receptive when she is with me. How would Friday night suit you?"

Friday would be just fine with Mr. Poole, and out came his billfold. Mama named a price that would have choked a regular fortune-seeking patron, but the rustle of paper money told me that he offered no complaint. Mama continued to murmur into the hall, where she wrapped him in his overcoat and found where his hat had slipped off its hook to the floor.

"That's her again!" cried Mr. Poole. "She's followed me here!"

"Oh, no. I don't think so," soothed Mama. "There aren't many spirits who dare to come here uninvited." She chuckled and opened the front door. Mr. Poole hovered on the step, not hurrying his good-bye.

I slipped to the window to examine this gent. He wore a wide-brimmed fedora, like a gangster, and pinstriped trousers. He patted Mama's arm more than once, he was that grateful. Finally, with a jaunty stride, he went off down Needle Street. I lingered in the hallway as Mama came back in, humming.

"Was that the gentleman who telephoned yesterday?" I still felt warm from listening to her flirtations. Mama pulled me into the front room and closed the door against the chance of Peg's ears catching my normal voice.

"Oh, yes," she said. "He was most certainly a gentleman."

I didn't like the way she said that. "What do you mean?"

"He's rich, he's well-spoken and his breath doesn't stink. He really believes that his dreadful wife is hovering like incense in a Catholic church. We're going to scare away her spirit," said Mama. "It will be quite an effort and take several tries. It will require investment on his part, but he will be very grateful in the end."

"How are we going to do that?"

"We start this week and take it step by step. On Friday evening we'll go to his home to perform a spirit banishment."

"But—but we're all set up here!"

"You'll have your toes, won't you? We can use the bell, and perform some hooey with earth from the garden. We won't do a full-fledged calling, just a quick contact. Mrs. Poole will speak just long enough to leave her husband craving more. I'll have him eating out of my hand before you can say 'Harry Houdini.' "

Oh, Mama must have felt brimful of confidence! Only so would she mention the great escape artist. To her mind, Harry Houdini was the devil. Houdini's mother had died a few years earlier and he'd tried to summon her spirit, using several different trance mediums. But he kept being tricked by fakes and had lost all faith that the spirit world existed. He'd since devoted his life to exposing frauds. Mama had nightmares about Harry Houdini appearing on our doorstep;

that was why we avoided publicity and stuck to Nowhere, New York.

She grinned at me, a rare and lovely sight. "It will be fun, Annie! A challenge. It's good for us to shake things up once in a while, keeps our wits lively." She looked down and realized that she was rolling Mr. Poole's paper money between her thumb and forefinger.

"This is only the beginning," she said. "I have plans for Mr. Gregory Sebastian Poole. . . ."

4

If you can make a cracking sound with your finger or toe joints, it is a sure sign that somebody loves you.

Mama dressed with great care on Friday evening and looked beautiful. She wore a shawl trimmed with feathers, making her seem as exotic as a wood nymph. I wore black, as I usually did for callings, the hint of mourning being a reminder of the solemn occasion. My skirt was specially rigged but not uncomfortable. My skin prickled and I was damp under the arms, but that was part of the thrill of performance.

I had assembled the supplies: a bell in a domed glass case, the second bell beneath my skirts, a silver sugar bowl with a matching pearl-handled scoop, a dozen candles with crystal saucers, a corked bottle of "cordial," fishing line, and smelling salts, just in case.

We arrived at Mr. Poole's house in a taxi, after sunset but while the sky still held pink light. According to our research, Mr. Poole employed five servants, and one of them was a gardener. There was privet hedge on either side of the drive and a tidy lawn bordered with flower beds, still bursting with asters this late in the season. A man wearing an old-fashioned frock coat led us into a large room where fancy French doors opened onto a terrace. A fire burned, trying to warm what the evening was cooling. The firelight danced against walls papered with patterns of twisting ivy.

Mr. Poole greeted Mama by grasping both her hands and kissing both her cheeks. Her eyelids fluttered charmingly. This was never my favorite part, watching Mama dally. I remained by the door, my face perfectly stupid.

"This is my daughter, Annie," said Mama, pulling me out of the shadows. "She is touched, as I told you." She paused while I sent him a crooked smile and wobbled my eye a couple of times. "The nuns at my school would have said that such a child was a blessing, Heaven-sent to test my faith. I believe that I receive certain communications because Annie is recognized as a creature undistracted by earthly concerns." Mama's golden tongue could turn even the blight of a hideous and demented child into a valuable possession.

Mr. Poole bowed slightly, without a wince or a shudder.

"Good evening, Annie," he said, as politely as if I were the town priest.

"Say hello, Annie," instructed Mama.

"Hello," I said.

"I noticed on the way up to the house," said Mama, "that you nurture a few late bloomers, like those sunny-looking purple asters."

"Christine planted those," said Mr. Poole.

"I hoped so," said Mama. "That is where we must dig.

Annie?" She spoke slowly and clearly. "Go to the garden, dear, and gather the earth."

Obediently, I unwrapped the silver sugar bowl and stepped into the twilit garden. I could hear the burbling of a fountain, though I couldn't see it. There was a smell of summer, of blossoms, even in September. As I crouched to dig, the bell slipped out of its pouch and jingled under my skirt. I crept behind the veranda post to adjust my rigging before going back inside. The way that bell sometimes misbehaved made me nervous.

"Have you a trusted servant who could join us?" Mama was asking as I came in. I held the sugar bowl reverently, like a chalice full of holy water. "Spirits feel more welcome," she said, "if there is more than one familiar face. I like to fill the table for a calling." There was nothing Mama loved more than an audience.

Mr. Poole pressed a button embedded in the mantelpiece. "I'll have my man, Douglas, come up, with his wife."

Douglas was the one who had answered the door. He inclined his head toward each of us in turn and then waited quietly for instructions. His wife, Norah, seemed fretful, as if she expected to be carried off by a ghost.

"Is there a piece of linen that your mistress might have handled?" Mama asked Norah. The maid went to a chest and lifted out a lace runner.

"No lace," said Mama quickly. "No holes. We need to contain the spirit."

Another cloth was produced and spread over the table. Mama had the lights dimmed and the candles lit. She placed the bell in its glass dome in the center of the table. She tipped it as she reached over to put it down, making it tinkle faintly. If everyone heard it ring ahead of the séance, they'd know it worked just fine. And sitting on the table, encased in glass, they'd expect it to be muted.

I perched on a stool at one end of the table, and Mama sat herself at the other. Mr. Poole sat beside her, and the servants sat across from them. No one but my mother was looking at me. I slid off my shoes. I blinked at Mama, signaling her to begin.

"Mr. Poole, do you have one of your wife's personal possessions with you, as I requested?"

"Ah, yes." He handed over a gold-link bracelet, medium weight, a gleaming rose gold that was pricier than the regular yellow variety. One perfect ruby dangled like a pomegranate seed, an opulent crimson drop. I watched Mama's face as she held it and saw her glow of pleasure.

"Let us all touch what Christine has touched."

Mama motioned to the "callers" to place their hands, palms up, on the table. She blew on the gold and passed it on, telling each of us to add our own breath. At my turn, I blew softly, clouding the ruby, as if I were sending a kiss. As eyes followed the bracelet, I gently released the bell from its inside pocket and held the clapper through the fabric of my skirt. When the bracelet came back to her, Mama dropped it into the sugar bowl, which she lifted above her head. With a sudden flick of her wrist, she tipped the bowl and sprayed dirt all over the table. The bracelet glimmered like a snake.

Norah gasped and struggled up, offended by the mess.

"Don't touch it," whispered Mama, and Douglas patted his wife back into her seat. Mama and I hummed quietly together until the room seemed to quiver. Then, *crack!* A sharp snapping sound made everyone jolt upright. I nearly giggled and flexed my other big toe. *Crack!*

"Christine? Christine Poole?" said Mama. "Are you with us?"

Without even a shiver above the surface, I jiggled my legs under the table. We heard the muffled ring and everyone stared at the glass dome, tickled by the hovering spirits.

"Oh, my!" said Norah.

With my feet tucked now on the rung of the stool, my knees were perfectly placed to make the table tilt, ever so slightly.

"Ahhh!" They were thrilled!

Mama's voice came again, but not her own voice this time. It was high and clipped, like the voice of a woman in a hurry. Choosing a voice is one of the trickier aspects of greeting a spirit. We have to guess, from what we know of a person's character, how she, or he, might sound.

"I want to speak with Gregory," said Mama. "Gregory, are you listening? I have something to say to you."

"Oh, my!" said Norah. "It's the mistress."

"You're haunting me, Christine," said Mr. Poole. "Why can't you leave me alone?"

"I am not at rest, Gregory. I wasn't ready to go. I didn't want to leave all my lovely possessions! You've now got everything my father worked so hard to give me."

"But you're dead, Christine! You're supposed to be at peace."

"My money is there! My house, my jewels, my dishes, my dresses."

"None of it can go where you are, Christine. I'm surprised you still care about such things. Aren't you beyond it all?"

"There's nothing to do here! I'm still waiting to learn where I'm going next."

"I don't understand."

"They can't send me to the Other Side until I've let go of Earth. You must help me, Gregory."

"But what can I do?"

"You have found the person to help. Give her whatever she needs. . . ." Her voice slowed and faded. "Caterina will guide you. . . ."

Mama's head slumped forward. I wobbled my knees to ring the bell again. Mr. Poole sat in a daze, his palms still flat on the table.

"Oh, my," announced Norah. "I'm coming over all strange." She half stood and then crumpled sideways and slumped to the ground in a heap.

"She's fainted!"

Douglas knelt beside his wife, fanning her face. I dove for our supply case, forgetting the bell, which jangled merrily under my skirt. I froze and looked around, catching Mama's glare. But Norah remained in her swoon, Douglas stayed on his knees, and Mr. Poole had jumped up to pour water from a carafe on the sideboard. Lucky, lucky, lucky.

I grabbed the bell through my skirt and used my other hand to dig in the case for the smelling salts. Of course I had to look clumsy, but for the lady's sake I made it swift, accompanied by several grunts. One whiff of the salts and Norah started up like a kitten under a tap. She tsked to find herself on the floor, and let Douglas lead her quickly out of the room.

The tender good-night between Mr. Poole and my mother took too much time and required my monumental patience. He was utterly indebted, as Mama had predicted, and ready to sign up for endless sessions: cards, palms, tea leaves, crystals, callings; all to banish the spirit—and, no doubt, the memory—of his dear late wife.

5

If you dream of seeing an idiot, you will have much discouragement and sorrow with your family members.

The knocker was clacking before Peg had arrived, so I scurried to open the door, crossing my eye on the way. It seemed early for anyone to be thinking about fortunes, but there were occasional emergencies when only a psychic would do.

It wasn't a customer. It was an enormous bouquet of yellow roses; twenty-four, because I counted. The delivery boy was Bradley Barker from the tenth grade, whose uncle owned Garden's Best, the florist shop. Poor Bradley had nasty pimples all over his face and neck. In my opinion, he was nearly as much an outcast as I was.

"They're the most expensive flowers we have," he said, handing them over with a small envelope. "And, no surprise, they're not for you. They're for your mother."

"Thank you," I slurred. I did not give him a tip.

"Aren't they lovely!" cried Mama when she appeared.

She inhaled the scent of the fresh roses with her eyes closed.

She read the card and passed it to me.

> May these light up your day
> as you have brightened mine.
> Will you do me the honor of dining
> next week?
>
> Gregory Poole

I'd seen that cunning look in Mama's eyes before, as she thought about where she might lead a romance. With Mama, it was part of the game.

It had never occurred to me that I might lose my sense over a boy. Mama didn't lose her sense. Except maybe the once that had resulted in me being here in the first place. Mama dealt the cards and always came out the winner. But I couldn't look at Sammy Sloane without my heartbeat getting the hiccups.

I began to get up early just to watch him walk past our door on his way to school. I'd figured out we were on the path from his house near the rail yards to the school at the bottom of the hill. I knew where he lived because I'd followed him home. Twice. As the days ticked by, I got bolder with my spying. One morning—with my breath coming out my ears, I was so on edge—I left the spot behind the lace curtain and moved to sit on the doorstep. I put on my new brimmed hat and tossed my hair. I was cheating on being daft, and Mama would strangle me if she knew.

I licked my lips and let them form a fetching smile.

33

Sammy Sloane wheeled along on his scooter and hopped off just as he came to the cracked sidewalk in front of our house.

"Hey," he said, eyebrows up, and smiling for a second before he realized it was me. He gave me a wave and took two steps. Then *whoosh*, back on the scooter and he was gone. I about swooned. He'd spoken to me.

I jumped to my feet for an ecstatic twirl. Then my spirits crashed and I kicked the door. There was no wonderful, black-haired boy on earth who wanted a wonky-eyed, chapped-lipped moron for a sweetheart.

The truth landed like a conker on my head. I would never have Sammy for a boyfriend. This boy who listened to his friends with his head tilted, and laughed at their jokes with bright, dark eyes; this boy who made my breath stop and my neck heat up as if his arm were already draped around it would never give me a moment's consideration, except as the loony girl.

I could feel my heart shriveling. I would never have a friend of any kind while we stayed in Peach Hill, where I was a joke and an imbecile. Mama and I would have to leave right away so we could start again somewhere else. We'd think of another ploy, and I could be myself instead of stupid. We must be nearly rich enough by now. We could find a little cottage in a different town, by the ocean, with a boardwalk and a concert in the bandstand on Sunday afternoons. Mama could stick to tarot cards, or retire, even, and—what would she do? We'd think of something. I'd go to school with clean hair and rosy lips and have friends. I'd meet another boy and someday, after a few tragic years of walking beside the white-capped sea, I'd recover from my heartbreak and forget about Sammy Sloane. But we'd have to go soon, before I was mortified more than I could bear.

I would tell Mama as soon as the customers were fed their fortunes and gone for the day.

Peg had roasted a chicken and hurried out to buy rice to go with it. While Mama read one last palm, I made some ginger tea and buttered slices of toast.

"Mama," I began when she came into the kitchen. "I have an idea."

"I've made a decision," said Mama at the same moment. She was so merry she was just about singing. "I like Peach Hill," she announced. "What do you think of moving into a house with a pagoda and a pond?"

"Mama, no!" I gaped at her. "Do you mean with Mr. Poole? Actually live with him? No! I was just going to tell you. We've made a mistake, and I think we should leave."

"Nonsense! We've only just arrived! This place is tingling with promise. I can feel it in my bones. Even the spirits are lively."

"Mama, you're talking about the spirits as if you believe they exist. We can't stay here. I don't want to be an idiot anymore."

"It won't be forever," Mama coaxed. "I have thought of a plan to make our fortune, once and for all. Mr. Gregory Sebastian Poole is a very rich man, Annie. I'm still a young woman. If I marry him—"

"Marry him?"

"Only for about five years."

"What?" I shouted. "Five years? No, Mama! You think I want to be an idiot for five years?" How could she suggest such a thing?

"I'll not be hollered at by my own child," snapped Mama.

"You won't listen if I don't holler!" I hollered. "You only ever think about you! What about me for a change?" I was mad as a trapped wasp.

Mama scraped back her chair and stood up, her hands clenched. "You hush at once." Her voice had an edge like a cleaver. But I couldn't stop myself.

"Is *Mrs*. Poole going to help your little plan? I suppose she's going to tell her husband to marry you and give you all her money? Why should you get to have a romance while I'm the ugly duckling with no hope of ever being kissed? I'll be drooling and stammering at your wedding. Is that what you want?"

Mama narrowed her cold, gray eyes, but I ducked past her and slammed out the door. I was bursting, I needed to scream.

"*Grrrack! Arrggerrack! Aarrrroooeeeeww!*"

I stomped along Needle Street, down Picker's Lane and around the square a dozen times, tears gushing. Maybe I was crazy after all. People hopped aside to let me pass, turning their faces away. I'd have grinned if I hadn't been so mad. Nothing like a loony on a rampage to clear the path.

It was the busiest time of day in Peach Hill. The two factories were changing shifts, the shops had just closed, kids were hurrying home not to miss the supper bell. The opportunity for chaos was enormous.

"*Rraaarrrgghh!*" I swung my arms like a windmill, not really caring what I hit. Most people sidestepped, but I collided with a woman struggling with a large market bag. She cursed me as vegetables bounced across the pavement. That pulled me up short, made me stop huffing long enough to inhale. I tried to help pick up the onions, but I was shooed away with an angry hiss.

Too late I noticed a band of high schoolers gathered outside the five-and-dime store, laughing and pointing at me. Not Sammy, thank goodness, but Delia, and a girl named Lexie, and Sally Carlaw, and Frankie Romero and Howie and another couple of boys. Howie jumped into step beside me, making ape noises, imitating the way I loped along. I wanted to evaporate!

I spun on my toes and aimed to whap him one upside the head. He dodged my palm, laughing, and then darted forward and tripped me! Tripped a retarded girl! I crashed to the ground, wrenching my ankle, my eyes and cheeks burning.

Now, finally, there was consternation from the onlookers. Someone scolded Howie for attacking me. Through half-closed eyes, I watched the group of boys creep backward and disappear, the cowards. My hair fell in a tangled curtain over my face. Someone produced a handkerchief; my face was wiped, my hair smoothed. I was fine, only shaking with fury, figuring out how to slink away. But then I heard a familiar voice.

"The fortune-teller's daughter?" It was Mr. Poole! "Is she ill?"

"She's an idiot, sir," said a child.

"She is sadly afflicted," confirmed a woman. "Generally, she's harmless, but that boy was riling her something dreadful."

"I'll see her home," said Mr. Poole.

"No!" I moaned, and rolled my eyeball so I could see.

Mr. Poole was inches away, with a stern gaze of concern. He had removed his fedora to fan my face and I caught a waft of coconuts.

"Do you remember me, Annie? I'm Mr. Poole."

Don't you dare marry my mother, I wanted to shout.

"No men!" I said. "No men!"

The circle of housewives laughed.

"No men, she said, the daft cluck!"

"Her mother's taught her right!"

"No men! Whatever next?"

"Nonetheless," insisted Mr. Poole.

"*No!*" I tugged myself out from under their hands and began to limp away, biting my lip against the pain in my ankle. Suddenly Delia bumped against me.

"This'll teach you," she whispered. "Stop coming near us. We don't want you around."

Mr. Poole caught up to us, and Delia slid away. I could feel my ankle swelling up; my knees and palms were raw and smarting; I was suddenly very cold. I hobbled toward home with Mr. Poole lurking behind. I was shaking with leftover sobs. As we arrived on Needle Street, he hurried ahead and had summoned Peg by the time I reached the door.

"Oh, Lordy," said Peg. "I could punch that boy right in the snout." She wrapped her arms around me, warm as a blanket, making me cry all over again. Peg loved me, not knowing I was smarter than she was. She loved me the way a mother was meant to love a child.

Mr. Poole followed us all the way into the kitchen.

Peg sat me down and unlaced my boot. Oh, oh, oh! The pain swelled to fill the room! I winced as I propped up my leg on another chair.

"Shouldn't she go to bed?" asked Mr. Poole.

"First I'll fix her some sweet tea."

"Ah, yes," he said, "for the shock."

His voice brought Mama running.

"Whatever has happened?" Mama took in the scene in an instant. "My baby's been hurt?"

She fluttered like an upset chicken and tried to stroke my hair. She knew how appealing a mother's worry could be. I jerked away, not willing to perform just then. Mr. Poole was telling Mama what he'd seen.

"Bullies! Tormenting a kitten!"

Peg put ice in a stocking to lay across my foot. She found me a woolly shawl and set the cookie jar next to my elbow.

"You rescued my darling heart!" cried Mama. I snarled.

"Help me pray!" She stood behind me, her hands like bricks on my shoulders. "Take away the pain from my little girl! Pray with me, Mr. Poole." I tried to shrug her off again.

"Perhaps you should let the child settle down," suggested Peg.

Mama led Mr. Poole out of the kitchen. "You've done a marvelous good deed today," I heard her say, her voice trembling but full of admiration. The door swung shut and I could hear only mumbles and whispers in the hallway. I held my breath, trying to decipher the actual words. Peg clanged about, making the tea, placing the cups just so on the tray.

"Do you think she'll want the tea in here, or will she make you move to serve it nice for him?"

"The ice is too cold, Peg," I said, shifting my foot.

I nudged the ice bag to the floor and leaned over to pick it up, pushing the door ajar while I was down there.

I saw what I was afraid I'd see: Mama pressed against Mr. Poole in the dim corridor, her cheek nestled against his chest, while he stroked her back with his large, comforting hand.

I screamed. Peg dropped the teapot and it smashed. I screamed again. And then the chance for freedom flashed like sheet lightning across my brain.

6

**Tea spilling from the spout
of the teapot while it's being
carried indicates that a
secret will be revealed.**

I threw myself to the floor, ignoring the shards of broken china and the puddle of scalding tea. I closed my eyes and screamed again. I stopped moving and stopped breathing. My ankle throbbed as if it would split open.

"What happened?"

"I don't know, ma'am."

"Is she alive?"

"I don't know, sir." Peg's voice was hardly a whisper. "She said the ice was too cold and then she begun that screaming and fell to the floor like a sack of sugar."

"Let's get her up out of this mess," said Mr. Poole.

I tensed all my muscles. Mr. Poole, Mama and Peg gasped. An excellent reaction. I took in a long, juddering breath. I flopped loosely on the floor, exhaled and lifted my eyelids. I gazed up at them calmly, with both my eyes. Peg was the first to realize.

"Annie?" She waved her fingers in front of my face, checking my focus.

"Hello, Peg," I said. No sloppy tongue, no waver, no twitch. "My ankle hurts like the devil and I seem to be sopping wet."

"Annie?" said Mama.

I kept looking at Peg, not wanting to risk Mama's gaze just yet.

"What's happened?" cried Peg, but answered herself at once. "She's cured, ma'am! I can tell by her eyes!"

I gave her my loveliest closed-mouth smile.

"Oh, ma'am!" cried Peg. "It's a miracle!"

"It's not a miracle," scoffed my mother. "Miracles don't happen like that, without saints and prayers and rolling thunder."

"But you did pray, Caterina," said Mr. Poole. "You laid your hands on her and begged that she be healed. This . . . this may be your doing. . . ." His voice dwindled in amazement.

But Peg began to squeal. "Stand up, Annie! Can you walk all right? Annie, stand up! It's a miracle, ma'am! You've worked a miracle!" Peg picked me up and spun me around, or tried, anyway. She started to laugh and so did I, giddy and jubilant.

Mr. Poole stood next to Mama, staring at me, adjusting his glasses. Mama's eyes locked with mine. I was certain she was calculating her options. But I had her. I watched her inhale and speak the opening lines of a new play.

"I suppose," she said, putting on a modest glow, "that with help from the stars above, it is possible that I have saved my precious daughter." She stretched out her hands, staring at them as if amazed by what they had done.

I had never written the script before, and here was Mama, following my lead! I was nearly dizzy with triumph. Peg squealed again and squeezed me. Mr. Poole squeezed Mama. Mama blushed, but she was watching me. I smiled. Deception ran in the family, after all. Mama had taught me to lie. She should be proud of me.

"I'm a bit tired," I confessed.

"Oh, my dear! It's straight to bed with supper on a tray!" Peg hustled me off to have a bath and snuggle under the quilt, where she brought me a soft-boiled egg and sugary tea.

When Mama had finally said good-night to Mr. Poole and came in to see me, I was asleep. Faking sleep was nothing after faking daft.

But she was sitting on the end of my bed in the morning.

"Aren't you the clever one," she said.

"Good morning to you, too," I said, sitting up, cramming the pillow behind my back, certain I was in for a long talk. But suddenly I was grinning, silly almost, knowing I had changed the world.

"Isn't it the most marvelous day?" I edged my ankle out from under the blanket. It was stiff and still quite puffy.

"The healing was an admirable idea, Annie, but clumsily executed and badly timed."

"Ah, Mama, can't you for once admit that I was clever? It worked brilliantly! Mr. Poole was astounded. Peg nearly died of happiness."

"It was not clever to waste a phenomenon on such a small audience! Naturally, I'd had the same idea," Mama said. Naturally, I thought. "But I was waiting to heal you when

43

it would work to our best advantage. This way, how do we benefit?"

"We benefit, Mama, because I can now be as clever as I am. I was tired of being stupid and ugly, especially if you plan to stick around here for a while."

She considered me. "You have overstepped yourself," she said, very quietly. "You are not to make any further decisions without consulting me."

"It was a spontaneous inspiration," I protested.

"There is no room for spontaneity in our lives, Annie. I'm surprised at you. Have you forgotten what happened in Carling?"

Meanwhile, Peg had been a gossip marvel. When I stepped outside with my hair brushed and my lips shiny with petroleum jelly, there was a gaggle of ladies already waiting to see Madame Caterina. We were suddenly the most popular attraction in all of Peach Hill. Every lady would be contributing to our house fund, and they all were watching me.

"It's her!"

"She's the one!"

"Look, two good eyes!"

I felt radiant, and then I choked. Sammy Sloane was leaning against the side of the building, scooter rocking under his left foot.

"Hey," he said. "I heard about you."

Oh, please let my voice sound calm! I thought. I will never have this chance again.

"Yup," I said. "It's a miracle."

44

7

The sound of bells frightens away demons.

"I always thought you were kind of pretty for an idiot," said Sammy, knocking the smile right off my face. This boy was fresh, maybe thinking he could take advantage, with me being so innocent. I glanced at the row of women waiting on line, all straining their ears to hear what I'd say.

"Whoa," I said. "My mama is a tough one and she won't like me talking to boys."

"She better get used to it," said Sammy. My grin crept back and nearly cracked my jawbone.

"Do you mind me asking," he said, "what it feels like?"

"What what feels like?"

"Being inside a miracle? Having actual contact with the spirit world? I've been thinking about you all night since my mother arrived home with the news. I think it's the most amazing thing I ever heard of!"

"Oh," I said. He'd been thinking about me? All night? He thought I was amazing? Or, at least, part of something amazing?

"Well," I said. "It's all so . . . so . . . overwhelming. I'm still trying to orient myself. I'll be happy to talk more the next time I see you."

"You'll be going to school now, won't you?" He might as well have poured ice down the neck of my blouse.

"School?" Oh, no! School!

"You know what school is?" he asked. "How much do you know about anything?"

"Not much," I said, taking the easy way out. "But I intend to be a fast learner. Why don't you tell me about school?"

"School is the place where kids have to go all day. They lock us in and drill us about numbers and the capital cities of places you're never going to go and dead people writing in books. And you sit at a hard little desk with scratch marks all over it made by the penknives of all the prisoners before you. And the teachers have special training with leather straps and hickory canes so they can whiz them through the air and make your heart jump and your palms sweat even if it's not you who forgot to memorize a poem about bluebells swaying in the breeze."

"Well," I said. "You make it sound awfully nice, but I don't think I'll be able to join you."

"That's what you think," said Sammy. "Wait till you meet Mrs. Newman and see if you're not begging to come to school."

"Mrs. Newman?"

"She's a truant officer with the nose of a shark on the scent of fresh blood. Her husband—"

"Mr. Newman?"

"Well, we call him Old Horse, actually, thanks to his teeth being the size and color of—"

"I get it," I said. "I've seen a horse."

"He's the janitor at Peach Hill Secondary and he's got this little dungeon down there in the cellar where Mrs. Newman puts the children who are trying to shirk school."

"She'll have to find me first," I boasted, heart galloping. We'd been talking for at least ten minutes and I hadn't stammered yet!

"Oh, shoot," said Sammy. The bells of St. Alphonse Church clanged across the square. "I'll see you tomorrow!" He pushed off on the scooter as if the hounds of hell were chomping at his heels. The bell rang nine times. Sammy was late for school.

And I was left with a crowd of eyes looking my way. Did it show? Could they tell I was wild for that boy?

"Good morning," I said.

"It's you, isn't it," said an old woman wearing a violet headscarf. "You've been healed."

I nodded.

"Your mother did that?"

"So it seems," I said.

"Can she cure my arthritis?" The woman held up hands like the claws of a crow, twisted over each other, bumpy and frail.

Oh, dear. I flinched. This was my fault. Real pain was something I didn't like to think about. But I'd turned Mama into a healer and here was a line of women with swollen joints and sore necks and aches in unmentionable regions.

They were maybe truly sick and should be consulting a doctor. We were about to exploit physical anguish instead of just foolishness and greed. Mama was suddenly a new hope, perhaps a last hope, for all these people and doubtless many more.

"I just want my pain to stop."

No! I wanted to shout, *No! Go away!* Taking money from someone who needed real medicine didn't seem right. But I swallowed. Loyalty. Loyalty to Mama.

I clasped my hands with a fervent sigh. "I pray that my mama can cure you as she has cured me! Perhaps I am a sign of many healings to come. But"—I lowered my voice—"as undeserving as I am, I may be the single chosen one. Perhaps only her great love for me and her years of prayer have made this happen."

The woman clutched at me with fingers like wintry twigs.

"I'll take the chance," she said. "I know that yesterday you were a babbling, cockeyed fool, falling down like a drunkard and making a scene. I'm a believer, hearing you now." She patted her handbag. "I've brought my savings," she said. "I'll give you whatever it takes."

Just what Mama wants to hear, I thought. Another sucker. And another brick in our dream house.

I pulled my sleeve from the old woman's talons and put my palms flat against her silky cheeks. "I'll add my touch to hers," I said. "May you be restored."

"She touched me!" cried the woman, lifting her hands toward the sky. Uh-oh. I imagined her neighbors on line pressing forward in a herd.

"I have to go!" I slipped back inside and leaned against

the door, breathing slowly. The sound of cracking china rang out from the kitchen.

"Oh, Peg!" Mama's voice was as sharp as a slap. "First the teapot and now the creamer!"

"It's not broken, ma'am, only a chip."

I could hear Mama's tongue clicking all the way down the hallway.

"Mama!" I called. "There is such a line outside you won't believe!" I bounded into the kitchen.

"What did you say, Annie, dear?"

That "dear" prickles my neck, the way it comes in handy in front of people but hides away when we're alone.

"There are people out front, Mama, lined up for Madame Caterina. Word of my—of your—healing is all over town. Did you tell anyone, Peg?" I gave her a poke.

"Well, I might have mentioned a time or two to a person or two last night that I'd seen a miracle before my very own eyes on the kitchen floor amongst the tea leaves I'd stirred with my very own hands."

Mama got the glinty eye that came along with any of her new ideas. "Good for you, Peg," she said. "Spread the word."

Peg smirked, pleased to have pleased Mama. "My father said my tea has sent him into fits for years," she said. "But anyone else I mentioned it to, they're all as thrilled as little children with the circus coming. Everybody wants to see you for themselves."

"Annie!" said Mama. "Peg is absolutely right!" She clasped her hands. "And what happens when the circus is coming?"

We stared blankly.

"A parade!" she cried.

"A parade," agreed Peg.

"A parade?" I was not thinking at Mama's pace today.

"You, darling!" said Mama. "You must spend the day on parade!"

I squinted at her.

"Walk around the square, have a sundae at the café, shop at the shops, show Peach Hill how you've changed. Show them all how clever and healthy you are. Here, take a few dollars." She stuffed money into my hand, showing me how seriously she meant this. "It's an investment," she added. "Go on, get out there." She nudged me out the door: a walking advertisement for Madame Caterina.

Peach Hill seemed like a different place now that I was allowed to have my wits with me. I liked the buzz of tittle-tattle following my every step. I pretended I was somebody famous, Mary Pickford or Buster Keaton. I could hear the ladies whispering, felt them rub up against me as if I were a good-luck amulet. They used to cringe if I came too close, and avert their eyes from the dribble on my lip, but today they made excuses to talk to me.

"Hello, dearie. What a joy to see you all fixed up!"

Old Miss Simmons:
More chins than born with.
Real pearls in that choker.

"Thank you, ma'am."

"Fine day, isn't it? You tell your mother I'll be around tomorrow with my sister, who gets hives."

50

Adelaide Goss:
Likes to wear husband's boots, by the look of it.
Son crossed over in the Great War.

"Yes, ma'am."

"Whatever next? A miracle in Peach Hill. I always knew you were a special child."

"Hello, Mrs. Ford." You never had a good thing to say about me, you old liar, except to show pity.

I spent every penny Mama had given me, knowing it was a rare opportunity. I bought a tin of talcum powder from the chemist—"June Rose"—and a paintbox, and a new book called *Black Beauty*. I lingered outside the window of Laraby Jewelry & Pawn Shop, always curious to see new wares.

But what was that? Sitting there in full view on a blue velvet tray was Mrs. Poole's bracelet, the one we'd passed about at the séance only last Friday. I would have known it anywhere, with that plum of a ruby. What was it doing here? Had Mr. Poole sold it for some reason?

I tried to treat myself to lunch at Bing's Café, but Bing's wife, Sadie, was quick to tell me, "On the house, darling, if you touch my sore knee."

"Happy to, ma'am. Delicious iced tea."

I hadn't decided whether to tell Mama about the bracelet at Laraby's when I burst in the front door, late in the afternoon, carelessly slamming it behind me. Mama hates a slam, especially when she's working. This time, it brought her out of the front room with a scary smile pasted on her mouth.

"Why, Annie, dear," she said. "You're home."

Dear? Who was with her? Not a customer, or the parlor door would have stayed shut.

"Come in, dear," said Mama. "There's someone here inquiring after your health."

I peered into the room. It was a woman, wearing a serge suit the color of lilacs. Her hair, faded yellow, was drawn back into a bun. Her hat sat on her knees with pansies popping up all over it.

"This is Mrs. Newman," said Mama. I recognized the note of poison in her voice. "She is insisting that you attend school, as of tomorrow morning."

"It's the law," said Mrs. Newman. "Not a personal whim."

My stomach began to churn. This was Mrs. Newman? This perfectly pleasant-looking woman with the silly hat was the shark Sammy had spoken about?

She wanted me to go to school?

Mrs. Newman was looking at me.

"I am overjoyed to have my child recovered," said my mother, stroking my cheek. "But she has only been well for a matter of hours. How can you imagine she is ready to attend school? She is not yet a normal girl."

Mrs. Newman's right eyebrow rose to a suspicious peak.

"She is not educated," Mama went on. "She has always been near me. Already the town bullies have plagued her. I fear she may have trouble if placed in a classroom with these same cruel children."

"Indeed, Mrs.—?"

"Madame," said Mama.

"Indeed, madame. It is my job to obey the law that states that all children under the age of sixteen must attend school.

Your daughter is apparently healthy and able. Her lack of learning is not a drawback but a challenge. However, you make an important point, that she is somewhat behind her peers in learning the fundamentals. She will be placed in the first grade under the instruction of Miss Carruthers and will—"

"But I need her at home!" Mama snapped. "She is a great help to me, and—"

"That is of no account. It is precisely to avoid the exploitation of children that the law was devised. The law states that all—"

"Oh, pish the law," said Mama.

"Excuse me," I said, so politely that even Mama stopped in surprise. "Mrs. Newman. I've been ill, or slow-witted, or, some say, idiotic. I'm not certain what you mean by school, exactly, but if it's a place where I'm to learn my letters and make some friends, why, it sounds wonderful!"

Mama snorted. I would not look at her. Mrs. Newman's eyes narrowed to blue slits; she didn't know she was handing me a ticket to freedom and adventure.

"I will accompany you to school in the morning," she said. Her gaze slid over my clothing. "You will need to look tidy and clean. Dark skirts are preferable, with a crisp blouse or trim sweater."

Mama actually snickered. "Crisp" and "trim" were not adjectives that applied to us.

"I don't have anything like that, ma'am."

"Do your best. I will be here at half past eight."

•   •

8

It is a lucky omen to meet the same person twice when you are out on business.

My mother believed in the power of costume; her dresses could best be described as foreign. She favored hot colors, orange and scarlet and peach. Her skirts were longer than the current fashion and folded about her like the robes of a rajah's wife. Her colored stockings arrived in brown packages through the post, and she bought them by the dozen. Mama would never dream of getting a bob—her luxurious black hair was part of her professional wardrobe.

Mama thought people were more likely to trust a spiritual advisor who wore a disguise.

"A priest, for example. Very dramatic, all in black. And look at the Pope! Now, there's a daring costume for a homely man."

Part of Mama's allure was to appear exotic, uncommon, a keeper of mystery and magic. She always looked ravishing, but as for me, I had never coped well with dresses. Mostly I wore silk smocks with loose, pajama-like trousers underneath. Mama ordered them from a Chinese lady in San Francisco, who also made fireworks. My only dress, the black one I wore for callings, had too many strings and pockets underneath to make it sensible for school.

"Since they're so damn insistent that you get an education, you can go naked as far as I'm concerned," said Mama with a dismissive sneer.

"I'll make you a skirt," offered Peg. "But I won't have time until the weekend."

"I suppose I could just wear my own clothes," I said. "The others already know what I look like. Who would I be trying to impress?"

Sammy Sloane's face appeared in my mind's eye, exactly the person I'd be trying to impress, but I couldn't admit that out loud. I imagined Sally Carlaw and Delia de Groot cackling behind their hands.

"You could borrow my Sunday skirt," suggested Peg. "Until Saturday. I'll make you something of your own then."

"Oh, Peg! Thank you!"

Sammy smiled at me while Sally and Delia turned away in jealous awe.

Back when I was six, when most children were in the first grade, Mama was La Bella Flora, the fortune-teller for Lenny's Famous Fun Fair. We lived in a real caravan, painted like a Gypsy wagon, and we traveled up and down the East Coast, pausing in towns for a couple of nights at a time. But that autumn, when I was six, Lenny broke his leg in a fall from the practice trapeze, and we stayed in a place called Turkleton for several weeks. All of us carnival kids went to the local school, to keep the authorities off Lenny's back. There were four others besides me: the nine-year-old Turino twins, who performed as savages and ate raw meat; Greta, the Fat Lady's dainty daughter; and Isabelle, my first friend, who was eight and could already speak four languages.

I was placed in the first grade.

My mother had taught me to read when I was three, so even back then I was bored to weeping with the Elson Reader. I was learning to juggle, and I knew the trick to lying on a bed of nails. I'd tried the trapeze and watched a man eat fire every night. First grade didn't hold much allure.

On what was to be my first morning at Peach Hill Primary, Mama sat home in a bath full of lavender-scented bubbles, daring me to go through with it. I walked out the door with Mrs. Newman and closed it firmly behind me.

Half an hour later, studying the rows of six-year-old heads in front of me, I cursed my own pride.

The letters of the alphabet marched across the top of the blackboard in Miss Carruthers' classroom. Paper oak leaves frolicked up and down the door frame.

"This is Annie, boys and girls. She will be joining us in room 102. Please make her feel welcome."

Everyone clapped politely. Miss Carruthers pointed to an empty miniature desk and I felt like a rhinoceros blundering my way to the back row. We stood to salute the flag and then bowed our heads and said a prayer. Little faces kept turning my way, sneaking peeks through fingers.

"Take out your maps, boys and girls," said Miss Carruthers. "We will first locate the Atlantic Ocean." I didn't have a map, so I looked out the window as we progressed through the Pacific, the Indian and the Arctic oceans in turn.

"You're the idiot, ain'tcha?" The boy in front of me scratched his armpit while he whispered at me. "Is that why you're in here?"

I gave him my coolest Mama stare.

"Well, is it?"

"Turn around," I said. "You're annoying me." He had a rash on the back of his neck, which I examined closely while the class tried to discover the difference between an ocean and a sea.

Ten minutes later, the boy twisted around again.

"Hey, idiot," he said. "You're a big, ugly baboon."

"Shush," I said.

"And you smell."

That was enough for me. I leaned over and yanked his ear just about off. He squawked like a chicken, and Miss Carruthers had us both in corners before I could spit. She said she'd attend to us later, which she maybe thought had me quivering with anxiety. From the corner, I listened to the lesson in arithmetic, learning to make change of a dollar in ten different ways.

I bounced my forehead gently off the wall in front of me. Even though I was there at my own request, it felt as though Mama had devised the perfect punishment for my announcing myself healed without consulting her. But I was a resourceful girl, wasn't I? I had the tools to fashion a different day for myself. . . .

During the lesson about using four nickels instead of two dimes to buy six oranges, I toppled over, just missing the corner of Miss Carruthers' desk. The teacher stopped mid-word, which had been my intention. Six-year-olds made a rewarding audience. They let out great gasps and hollers of excitement.

"She fainted!"

"She's dead!"

"Is there blood?"

"I see blood!"

"Did her brains come out?"

"She's got no brains! She's an idiot!"

"Move back, boys and girls. She needs air." Miss Carruthers hovered above me, brushing the hair off my face.

"Daniel, fetch some water, please," she said, and feet clattered out of the room.

"She's an idiot," I heard again. "Her mother is the fortune-teller. She's a moron."

"Not anymore," said someone else. "Now she's smart enough for the first grade."

"Oh, Daniel, thank you." The teacher spoke to her helper. "Thank you. Oh! No! Daniel!" The warning came too late. Instead of delivering the cup of water into Miss Carruthers' hand, Daniel had tossed it full force on my head. The surprise made me jerk to life. Another thrilled chorus buzzed through the children.

"Can you walk, dear?" asked Miss Carruthers.

"I think so." Absolutely, certainly, just open the door.

"You'd best be off home, then," she said, washing her hands of me. "Have a nice rest. We'll see you in the morning." Her smile couldn't hide her hope that I would have a relapse and never again appear in room 102.

* * *

I had not expected to miss being an idiot, but even lurching aimlessly around town had been better than first grade. I felt no need to hurry home now. Mama didn't have to know yet that she'd been right.

Sometimes I liked the leafy square and Bing's Café and the bustle of business. And sometimes I liked the alleys that ran between the main streets in the town, paths to the back doors of the shops for deliveries and snoopers.

The bins behind the greengrocer's stank of rotting vegetables. I paused at the Blue Boy Bakery, where warm air billowed out, smelling of fresh bread. I peeked in the back window of the Lucky Ladies Fashion Boutique, wondering if I would ever have cause to pass through its door, to bring home something nestled in pink tissue paper.

A moment later I heard a holler and a bang and then pounding footsteps. I was bumped to one side as somebody hurtled past. The baker's boy ran toward me, shouting and waving his fists.

"It wasn't me," I said at once.

"Well, I know that," he spat. "It's the brat that comes every day. Every day, I swear, she sticks her paws through the door and swipes buns straight off the cooling rack. Every damn day."

"I'd close the door, if I were you," I said.

"No, you wouldn't." He looked scornful. "It's hotter than hell in there. You'd curl up like a parched fish if you closed the door." He kicked a garbage bin on his way back to work.

I crept farther down the alley, wondering where "she" had tucked herself. Aha! Behind Murray's Hardware, she was crouching next to crates of roofing shingle. She looked disarmed for only a flash, until I said, "I won't tell." She stood up with her hands on her hips, daring me somehow.

I'd guessed already, of course, though I hadn't seen her since the day in the square when Sammy Sloane had first appeared. She wore the same shabby overalls, and her dark hair hung past her shoulders, shaggy and uncombed. She was nearly my age, I thought, but smaller than me, lean, almost bony. Her face was sharp, like a canny dog's. There wasn't the faintest friendly spark in her glare. She had a bun in each fist, with bites out of both.

"You do that so he can't take them back if he finds you?" I asked. She took another bite.

"You hungry?" I said.

"None a yer business," she said. I shrugged. She shrugged back and pushed past me. By the time I turned around, she was darting down the alley, two shops away, and then gone.

I dashed after her at once but couldn't see where she'd left the alley. Beside the bakery or farther along? Out on Main Street, I saw a blur of denim and a hand snatching an apple from the pyramid outside Carlaw's.

I leaned against a brick wall, catching my breath. Who was that girl? Aside from the sneakiest thief and the fastest runner I'd ever seen? I didn't like to be outsneaked or outsmarted, and I vowed that it wouldn't happen next time.

A kerfuffle arose outside the greengrocer's. One of the clerks, wearing a white apron, waved his hands in the air while he spoke to a short policeman. The officer looked up and down the street, spotting me at once. The clerk jerked his finger in the opposite direction, where the thief had run, but I didn't wait to see whether he was listened to. I was a school-age girl hanging about for no good reason.

Without a second's thought, I scooted into the park, across the square and up the stone steps of St. Alphonse, where the huge door stood open and welcoming. I peered behind me to see that I wasn't being followed. But instead of venturing out just yet, I sniffed the incense and went inside.

I hadn't spent much time in churches; I didn't understand the secret ceremonies. But it seemed like the best place for a spirit calling I could think of, with the candlelight flickering, celestial voices humming, and pale, plump angels pictured all around. Just entering the eerie gloom, I felt as if I'd swallowed holiness and was on my way to the Other Side.

I sat on one of the gleaming pews and bent my head in case anyone was watching from some stone cranny off to the side. If I believed a prayer would be answered, what would I pray for?

A home of our own, perhaps? We should be able to get that with hard work, not by wasting a prayer.

To meet my father? Well, maybe. But there might be a good reason that Mama had never bothered to make that happen. To have my mother cup my face in her hands and tell me she loved me? That would require a full-blown miracle, the kind that people came to us for.

I wondered, on the way home, if Peg might have made a stew for supper, with rich, meaty gravy. Peg was a much better cook than either Mama or me. Mama favored suppers that didn't involve cooking—plates of cheese and grapes, or Campbell's Cream of Celery soup with crackers and a sliced tomato. In Mama's opinion, those new soups that arrived in cans, without anyone's having to chop and boil for half a day, were the most glamorous addition to the modern kitchen. If I had been looking after myself, I would have eaten scrambled eggs every meal, with bacon or without. But Peg made real meals, with roasted meat and potatoes whipped with butter and green beans sliced sideways, which she called French. I was dreaming up the perfect dessert of peach cobbler when I opened the door and *bam!* Like characters in a terrible play, Mama and Mrs. Newman were standing in the hallway just as they'd been the day before at about the same time.

9

To prevent an unwelcome guest from returning, sweep out the room she stayed in immediately after she leaves.

"Well, there you are!" cried Mama. "Wherever did you disappear to? You've given us such a scare!" Danger swirled in the air like a mist. "Mrs. Newman tells me there was an incident at school. That you had a bad turn?"

Peg appeared at the kitchen door, her face showing relief as bright as lipstick.

"She played truant on her first day," pronounced Mrs. Newman firmly.

"Annie, dear," said Mama. "Come into the front room and sit down." The room was spotless, ready for that evening's calling. "I am expecting clients at any moment," she told Mrs. Newman. "I am conducting a séance. There are several seekers coming to call on their loved ones who dwell beyond the Curtain of Death."

"Your daughter was truant on her first day of school."

Mama adjusted the lace at the window. "Well, naturally, I'm terribly worried about Annie." Her smile was quite convincing. So real, in fact, that I knew she was gloating. If I'd left school after stubbornly insisting on going, then she'd won another round.

"She attacked a boy—an innocent six-year-old boy—and then fled from the school at the first opportunity."

"I'm sure Annie didn't intend to hurt the child, did you, darling?"

"That innocent six-year-old boy called me a smelly idiot, Mrs. Newman. And a big, ugly baboon." I spoke with a tremble. "I'm very sensitive about my former condition and not quite used to being with other children yet. I did not mean to create a disturbance. The teacher forced me to stand in the corner—"

Mama shook her head in disgust.

"—and I felt a terrible dizziness coming on and—"

"Miss Carruthers did report that you fainted," admitted Mrs. Newman.

"You fainted?" Mama repeated.

"All the more reason that your absence this afternoon has been noted as willful truancy," said Mrs. Newman. "The faint was clearly a ploy to excuse—"

"I didn't realize that I'd fainted," I said slowly. Inspired by my moments inside St. Alphonse Church, I felt a new idea swelling within me. "I can't even tell you where I've been. I haven't noticed anything outside myself."

Oh, such an idea!

"Where my body has been is a mystery. But my soul has

been transported!" Even Mama had never had an idea like this one. "I heard music, but it seemed I was enveloped in a dark shroud."

"For four hours?" Mrs. Newman bit off her words as if they were a gingersnap.

"Mama!" I fell to my knees and buried my face in rose-colored chiffon. "Oh, Mama, I believe that I have been possessed by a spirit. She entered my mind and took control of my limbs. I seemed to be watching from a distant place as she took me on a remarkable journey."

Mama shook her leg and pried me loose with her hands.

"Whatever are you babbling about?" All effort to be gentle and concerned had turned into irritation.

Mrs. Newman joined her. "This is the most ridiculous spewing of poppycock I have ever encountered! Get to your feet this instant, young lady!"

I tipped my head so that only Mama could see my face. I winked. The perfect partner, she rallied in an instant.

"Tell me again, Annie, dear," she said. "Speak more slowly."

"I received the spirit of a girl named Gwendalen," I said. "I felt her slip into my body, as though I were a merino sweater. She told me she was born in 1214. Or, well, she didn't exactly tell me, because she didn't speak using words. She seemed to transfer her thoughts to me. . . ."

"Bosh!" said Mrs. Newman.

"She lives in a convent," I continued. "She showed me scenes from her life, as though I were sitting at the moving pictures. Her father was very cruel and sent her away when he could not find her a husband. She said that if I provide her with ink and parchment she'll communicate through me to write down her story."

"What utter nonsense!" snorted Mrs. Newman. "I have never encountered such drivel! Your imagination borders on insane. Missus—Madame—how can you put up with this?"

"It is not unheard of, Mrs. Newman," said Mama quietly, "when there has been a cataclysmic occurrence such as the healing of my daughter, that other magnetic forces come into play. She could easily be a conduit! The living, breathing conduit for a spirit who is trapped between worlds." Mama's voice rose with excitement. "If this is the case, we can all rejoice! If Annie has been selected as a vessel of spiritual power, it is something to celebrate!

"Peg! Peg!" Mama began to shout.

Mrs. Newman's mouth dropped open in a gape of disbelief. "Both of you," she muttered. "Like mother, like daughter." She stepped away from us, her hands up as if to fend off an attack.

"Yes'm?" Peg appeared from the kitchen, drying her hands on a tea towel.

"Please find paper and a fountain pen in the drawer of my writing desk and bring them to the front room."

"Yes'm."

"You're going to indulge your disobedient and truant daughter in this way?"

"Gwendalen said parchment, Mama."

"This is absurd," said Mrs. Newman.

"She likely didn't have paper, darling heart," said Mama. "In the twelve hundreds, did you say?"

There came a knock at the door.

"Oh!" cried Mama. "The callers are here already. Peg! Never mind the paper! Peg! Answer the door!"

"I'll get it, Mama." I stepped around Mrs. Newman and opened the door. Two young women were there, both wearing wool jackets with thick raccoon collars turned up. The sky had turned gray since I'd come in, and a blustery wind was blowing. Behind the ladies was Mr. Poole, smirking like a well-fed Persian cat. I glanced at Mama. Did she think he was handsome?

"Hello, Annie."

"Come in," I said. Peg bustled up to help with the coats.

"This is the miracle child," Mr. Poole told his companions. "Observing her now, it's hard to remember that she was no better than a drooling moron last week."

If only I could arch my eyebrow like Mrs. Newman's!

"I hope I have not offended you, my dear. It was none of your own doing. And now, you see? Here you are, greeting us like a perfect little hostess."

"We've had the most thrilling thing happen," gushed Mama. "Just this afternoon, it seems that my Annie has had the honor of becoming a vessel for a spirit caller."

She was greeted with a trio of blank faces.

"There are rare occasions," Mama said, trying to explain the unexplainable, "when a restless spirit seizes the chance to inhabit a living person and gives voice to centuries of wisdom and poetry—"

"Well, well," said Mr. Poole. "Another marvel."

"Please, step in," I said.

"This is my wife's niece, Claudia Weather," said Mr.

67

Poole, putting his hand on the shoulder of the taller girl. Taller because her shoes had higher heels. She also wore too much rouge, like buttons painted on her cheeks. "Noisy," my mother would say.

"Good evening, Miss Weather." I bobbed a curtsey and backed up, trying to make room in the crowded hallway.

"This is Claudia's good friend, Sylvia Torn, who lost her husband in the Great War. She's visiting from Springfield."

"Oh, dear," I said. "That's the saddest thing I ever heard." We naturally had no file on someone from another town. Mama widened her eyes at me in a silent command; I had two minutes to extract something useful from her. "What a pretty ring," I gushed. "Were you newlyweds?"

"We were married four months and nine days before he went overseas. In New Orleans. That's where we were from."

"I'm so sorry."

"But I couldn't bear to go back there after he died, so I'm trying out a new place. I just . . ." She shrugged. "I keep expecting to wake up and still be Buddy's girl. I just can't seem to get on with things."

Mrs. Newman would not budge an inch the whole time Peg was taking the coats. It got to be awkward with her just standing there. I'd have to introduce her.

"This is Mrs. Newman," I said. "Mr. Poole, Miss Weather, Mrs. Torn."

"Will you be joining us for the calling, Mrs. Newman?" asked Mr. Poole.

"No," I said.

"No," said Mama.

"I don't think—" said Mrs. Newman.

"Oh, please stay," said Mr. Poole. "We would be delighted to extend the circle. If you haven't seen Madame Caterina before, you must join us." He was such a gentleman that she would have seemed downright rude to say no. "It's sure to be a remarkable experience."

Mrs. Newman smiled a half-smile and allowed Peg to take her coat too; her thin woolen coat without a trace of fur, not even rabbit, on the collar.

10

If you use the same pencil to write a test that you used to study for the test, the pencil will remember the answers.

"Have you been to a séance before?" I asked as Mama ushered everyone into the front room. The young ladies shook their heads.

"We never know who will be waiting on the Other Side to greet my mother," I explained. "She sends the message through and hopes to reach the callers' departed loved ones, but the connection is fragile and occasionally broken." I had to tell them this in case there was a perilous moment or an awkward question and Mama had to end the séance abruptly.

"How did you first know you had the second sight, Madame?" Miss Weather asked.

"Oh, even as a child," said Mama, "I heard voices and saw what I now know were visions. I was eleven or twelve before I discovered that not everyone was able to see beyond the place and time where their earthbound bodies dwelt. My cousin, Timothy, died of diphtheria, but he still spent his evenings in my room, playing Hide the Button and begging for ghost stories." She always gave a melancholy laugh at this point in the recollection. "Poor little mite didn't know he *was* a ghost."

I wouldn't want to read the book where Mama found that muck, but it often inspired wet eyes. Mr. Poole's niece and her friend were likely softies. Mrs. Newman, however, looked as tough as a cowboy's backside.

I lit the candles, set in sconces on the walls and in crystal saucers on the windowsill. The only electric illumination was a standing lamp, which Mama kept draped with a pink scarf so it cast a glow of sunset in one corner. Most mediums preferred to perform in complete darkness, but to us that screamed of tricks. Mama said "Seeing is believing," so we kept the lights turned on, a little.

The seating arrangement was a delicate matter. Mama had her chair and I had mine, already rigged as needed. But it had to seem to the customers that I simply slid into the last empty seat. Once everyone was sitting down, I slipped off my shoes and looped the transparent fishing line around my ankle as I pretended to scrape my chair into position. That was the official opening of our routine. Mama admonished me, as she always did: "Annie, you'll scare off the spirits. Be careful, dear heart!"

One of the ladies giggled, Miss Weather, I think. A nervous laugh is common at the beginning of a calling. We try to have them crying by the end. I was nervous that day, with Mrs. Newman sitting there looking downright leery.

"We must warm the connection," Mama began. "Please place your hands on the table. . . ." All hands were obediently laid on the gleaming walnut surface. We gave a minute to let people settle, to sit quietly in the flickering light, to wonder what would happen next.

Mrs. Torn sat beside me with her fingers spread wide, showing off ragged nails. She must chew them like toast. Mrs. Newman seemed to be gripping the table, the sinews taut on her long fingers. Mama's hands were elegant, with beautifully shaped nails. The tips of her fingers drummed gently on the wood; she was impatient to get started. Miss Weather, across the table, had pulled off her gloves as we sat down, revealing a wart near the tip of her ring finger. Mr. Poole sat next to his niece. His hands were large, with a light crop of dark hair below each knuckle. How could Mama consider marrying him? He had hairy fingers! He sat bolt upright, perhaps more excited than anyone else.

"Take the hands of your neighbors to form a circle," said Mama. Mama did a lovely séance, I must say. The candles were placed just so, to keep a golden gleam on her face, highlighting her cheekbones and catching auburn flecks in her dark hair.

"Let us hum together," she said. "It will improve our chances of entry into the spirit world."

Most people were self-conscious and needed to be shown. Mama began, as always leading the way. Of course I joined right in with her, my hum soft and steady, on a higher note than hers. Mr. Poole started up, deep and rolling. He likely sang bass in the church choir. Miss Weather and Mrs. Torn were a bit meek with their contribution, and Mrs. Newman made no sound at all. Her eyes stayed intently on Mama, which was certainly best for me. The candles wavered, not by my doing but just because of air currents. The flicker made the two young women gasp and Mrs. Newman roll her eyes.

It worked best to keep the hum going strong until people stopped twitching, until they were nearly bored. Mama's voice got subtly higher and began to falter, as if she were deciding which note to continue. Her eyes closed halfway. That was my signal.

Crack! Ladies always jumped at the sharp snap below us, or was it coming from the corner of the room? Squeals were stifled. Another *crack!* Mrs. Newman leaned over slowly to look under the table. There was nothing for her to see except legs and boots and my stockinged feet, playing with my shoes. I waited until she was upright and then *crack!* I knew she was puzzled, but she held her face blank. Mama jerked abruptly, as if she had collided with some force invisible to the rest of us. She recovered quickly but remained slumped and began to speak in a husky voice, completely unlike her own.

"I am standing at the Gate to Beyond," she said. "There is quite a crowd to greet us here today. There is a fellow in uniform, wanting to speak to Sylvia Torn."

Mrs. Torn shrieked. She dropped my hand and Mrs. Newman's. Her fingers flew to her mouth.

"He's waiting, Sylvia Torn. Are you ready to hear him?"

"Yes!" she bleated. "Yes, I am!"

I waggled my foot, tugging the fishing line to make the pink kerchief hanging over the lamp flutter wildly for a moment. Rosy shafts of light flew across the ceiling, and the candle flames danced. Mama's voice altered pitch and took on a faint Southern twang.

"Sylvie?" she said, guessing.

Mrs. Torn nodded urgently and moved her hands from her lips long enough to whisper, "Buddy?"

"Who else?"

"Buddy!"

"How's my girl?"

"Oh, Buddy! I miss you!"

"Don't you worry about me anymore. I'm doing just fine over here. But it's time for you to buck up, my girl. Time to move on."

"Oh, Buddy! I can't live without you!"

"Sure you can! You're my girl, aren't you? Tell you what I think. You need a job," said Buddy.

Mrs. Newman made a sound, but Mama kept going.

"In a shop, maybe, or a café? Get out and meet some new people, maybe even a fella, eh, Sylvie? You're too pretty to mope about all day, biting your fingernails!"

"What?" Mrs. Torn curled her fingertips into fists.

"I love you, Sylvie." Very faint.

I cracked my toe joint again quickly, hoping to limit the sobs.

"Buddy's gone," said Mama's husky voice. "Handsome fellow, wants the best for you."

"Yes," breathed Mrs. Torn.

"But there's someone else here who won't wait a moment longer. She insists on speaking to Gregory Poole."

"Christine?" said Mr. Poole.

"Gregory? Gregory? Is that you?" Mama's voice was high and querulous, the same one she'd used in his fancy dining room.

"It has been a quiet week," said Mr. Poole. "Thank you, Christine."

I had a sudden vision of her bracelet nestled on velvet in Laraby's window. I hadn't told Mama, but now I looked at Mr. Poole more closely. Was he really thanking her for her jewelry?

"I've been resting," said Mrs. Poole. "Watching you. I'm trying to decide what I think of your new friend."

"Oh, well, ah . . ." Mr. Poole was embarrassed and confused. His wife was speaking through the mouth of the very friend she was being rude to!

"And I've noticed that you haven't been to visit my grave, Gregory." Mr. Poole squirmed as Miss Weather looked up sharply. Good guess, Mama! "It could use some attention. What will people say?"

"Ah, well, you're right, Christine. I'll order fresh flowers tomorrow."

"No woman alive will feel affection for a man who doesn't honor his deceased wife."

"Ah, thank you, Christine. Is there anything you'd like to say about the business?"

"Watch carefully for signs, Gregory," said Mrs. Poole. "You haven't heard the last from me."

Mama loved to tack that on with wealthy clients. Even if they loathed their dear departed, they could never resist hearing more as promised. Mama started to hum, ever so quietly, so I knew to crack my toe again.

Suddenly there came a thud, and it wasn't me this time. I was the only one who jumped, because the others didn't know we were at the end, didn't realize we were waiting for Mama's "fall" out of trance.

Instead we heard her husky voice again. "There's quite a vision here now. She's an ancient soul indeed and seems to be wearing—is it called a wimple? She's here for Annie."

"Wha—?" One syllable escaped before I gathered my wits. I settled my hands back to the table. All eyes were on me.

"This is Annie," I called out.

There was silence, then a thump.

"She cannot speak," said Mama. "She wants parchment and ink."

"Parchment?" said Mr. Poole.

I looked around wildly. Peg had been distracted by the guests' arrival and had not brought the paper. We couldn't call her in the middle of a séance!

Mrs. Newman removed her hands from the circle and groped beneath her seat. She dragged her bag onto her lap and pulled out a notebook, which she laid flat on the table. She riffled through it, past columns and lists to a blank page toward the back. Mama was back to humming all the while. Mrs. Newman produced a sharpened pencil and placed it in the center of the book.

"There," she said. "The parchment of 1924."

Mama's eyes stayed half lowered, and she kept humming for a bit before speaking. "She wants Annie to hold the writing implement."

"Tell her it's called a pencil," said Mrs. Newman, sounding peevish. The notebook was passed to me and I picked up the pencil, awaiting inspiration.

I took a breath and threw my head back and then forward

as if someone were throttling me. I shuddered a tremendous shudder and began to write.

My name is Gwendalen of Stone House, I scrawled. *I am daughter to Arne the Vast and Elbecca of Tune.*

"What's she writing?" whispered Miss Weather. "What does it say?"

"I can't quite see," said Mrs. Torn.

"Well, lean over! Read it aloud!"

I kept going.

My oldest brother, Horehound, has gone to be trained for the wars. The next brother, Matts, is gone to a monastery. I reached the age of fourteen and could not be married easily as I am homely and tall. I angered my father in many ways. I was sent away from my home, nine days' journey with a mule, to join the convent at Craighn, the order of Saint Lucy, patroness of blind people and writers. . . .

Mrs. Torn began to read aloud over my shoulder, which made me falter for a moment, but I quickly resumed my masterpiece. She caught up to me and then had to wait for every word.

Although it is not usual for a damsel to be a scholar, the sisters recognized my gift and permitted me to read the Holy Book and to compose odes of a dramatic nature. Until my father, Arne the Vast, had occasion to visit the convent. He was displeased with my occupation and this led to my grim death.

Mrs. Torn stopped reading. "Oh! Poor thing!"

I kept writing.

Now I wander the heavens seeking outlet for my verses, until today, when I am joyous to enter my spirit into the willing vessel of young Annie, newly healed and an open soul.

I stopped. Mrs. Torn stopped. The candle flames quivered. I threw my head back and then forward, steeling myself for the thwack of pain as my forehead smacked the walnut tabletop.

Miss Weather sighed. Mr. Poole stood up and came around the table to pat my shoulder.

"Ooh, I was hoping we'd hear how she died," said Mrs. Torn.

Mama went into her crooning song while I shivered and twitched, my hand still gripping the pencil and outstretched across the page. The customers, normally afraid to move for some time at the end of a calling, clustered around me where I sat, my head still pressed to the polished wood.

My mother spoke in her own voice.

"What has happened here? Annie? Is Annie all right? Peg?" She flung open the door. "Peg? Come here at once! Bring a damp cloth!"

I shuddered once more and sat up, rubbing the bump on my forehead.

"Oh, thank goodness!" breathed Mrs. Torn.

"Caterina." Mr. Poole followed Mama to the hallway. "Your daughter is awake."

Peg scurried in. I was blotted with a dripping tea towel, and the customers clucked with relief. Only Mrs. Newman hadn't prodded me or expressed concern for me. From the corner of my eye, I saw her retrieve the accounting book holding the pages dictated by Gwendalen.

Peg bundled the ladies into their jackets. Mr. Poole put a hand on Mama's arm. "Thank you, my dear. That was extraordinary." He handed her an envelope, which she tucked neatly away. "Was it everything you hoped for, Sylvia?"

Mrs. Torn clasped her hands. "Oh, Madame! I have dreamt of Buddy every night for five years, and he never spoke to me so nice as he did tonight. Thank you with all my heart!" She followed her friend outside.

Mr. Poole leaned in closer to Mama. "I have a proposition to make, my dear. I would very much like to offer my services as a manager for your talents, and those that your daughter is now displaying. May I take you out for dinner very soon to discuss the possibilities?"

Mama smiled at him, tossing her hair ever so slightly. "Gregory, you've made two tempting offers!"

Manager? We didn't need a manager!

He kissed her hand and bowed his way out the door. She turned her attention to the remaining guest.

"Thank you for joining us this evening, Mrs. Newman." Mama swept her arm wide as she held the door open.

"It was . . ." Mrs. Newman paused, her notebook held against her chest under folded arms. "It was eventful," she said. "And most gratifying to know that young Annie has quickly mastered her letters so well. I feel confident that she could succeed, even in the tenth grade. Let's see how that works, when she comes back to school in the morning."

With those words of doom, she whisked herself off into the night.

11

**In ancient Egypt, when a cat
in a private house died
a natural death,
all the residents shaved
their eyebrows.**

When I went to tenth grade I would be in the same room as Sammy Sloane for six hours a day. The anticipation was almost more than I could bear. But this was not the excuse I used to appease Mama. She was irked that we had come up with such a clever new character and I was being dragged off to waste my time at school.

"It might be good for business," I said. "It's risky to depend on Peg for fresh gossip. Her sources are patchy, and she's not reliable when it comes to details."

"My customers are not generally attending high school," said Mama.

"But who is more likely to reveal a dirty family secret than a sulky fifteen-year-old?" I asked.

"I hope you do not include yourself in that description?" said Mama.

Why answer that?

"You may go on a trial basis," she said. "As long as it does not interfere with my plans."

I didn't remind her that Mrs. Newman had no interest in Mama's plans. She obeyed the law.

Peg made me an egg salad sandwich, wrapped carefully in waxed paper, and packed it with two pieces of shortbread and a bottle of milk.

"If you want to carry it home and eat your lunch here with me, you'll be welcome, of course," she said. "But you might make yourself a friend. You'll want to sit in the yard there at the school, like I used to do, for the noon recess. There will be girls with skipping ropes, boys with balls. You'll see! A whole crop of new friends."

"Thank you, Peg." I kissed her. It was kind of her, but so unlikely that I might have a friend to share cookies with after three hours of high school. I'd find a place to eat and make up stories for Peg.

I wore her skirt again, with a fuzzy white sweater from Mama's trunk. I dithered while I rearranged my hair—side part or center part? "Bump into" Sammy Sloane or walk alone? Would it be smart or dumb to show up on the first day with a boy? Would he even want to walk with me? Might be one thing in front of my house and quite another in front of all the kids at school.

I chose side part and walk alone. But I'd forgotten about Mrs. Newman. She was waiting on our doorstep, wearing gloves and a scarf that morning, along with her flowery hat. She looked me up and down. She pursed her lips but did not comment. Peg gave me a squeeze before I set out. My mother had chosen not to bid me good-bye.

I trotted beside Mrs. Newman, scrambling to think of conversation. The weather? That would last one minute, perhaps. A humorous reference to wearing Peg's skirt? Mrs. Newman might not like to hear me complain.

Mrs. Newman thought of something first.

"You may encounter suspicion, Annie," she said. "Or teasing. But you may not respond as you did yesterday. I'm depending on you to behave in a mature and responsible manner."

"I'll consider that, Mrs. Newman."

She actually laughed. Then she stopped me in the street and put her hands on my shoulders.

"You're a smart girl, Annie Grey. Perhaps not quite as smart as you think, but clever enough. I'm not sure what dubious deeds your mother has led you into, but it's not actually my business. My business is to keep you in school. That's the law. I'm paid to hunt down truants. If there's another law you're breaking, I may trip across it and be forced to make a report under some heading or other, but until then you need to be at school every day, no matter what. If the other students give you a thrashing and leave you bleeding on the pavement outside Bing's, I'll pay attention, but until then, you're on your own, whatever the level of mockery might be. I'm sure you're clever enough to think up a few names to call them back."

She clapped my shoulders briskly, bucking me up. We walked on a few paces.

"Perhaps Gwendalen of Stone House could inspire you in

this," she said. "Her father, Arne the Vast? Now, that is creative naming." She didn't look at me, but she chuckled.

I smirked briefly, proud to have succeeded in amusing her. But as we walked, the silence expanded. She was not fooled by Mama's act. Should I be protesting? Trying to convince her? I'd never had prolonged contact with a scoffer. How dangerous might she be? Did she really not care, except about school? If I mentioned my worries to Mama, she'd have her claws out in a flash. But . . .

When we arrived at Peach Hill Secondary School, Mrs. Newman took me straight to the office of the principal, who was nowhere in sight. Mrs. Newman explained briskly to the secretary that I was new. The woman polished her glasses and sharpened her pencil before looking up at us.

"Name?"

"Annie Grackle," I said, following my mother's edict, "Never use your real name." Mrs. Newman did not flinch, aside from a quiver in her eyebrow.

"Address?"

"Sixty-two Needle Street."

"Father's name?"

"Unknown."

The secretary blushed to the roots of her bleached and strawlike hair.

"It was an episode of passion," I added carelessly.

"That is quite enough, thank you," said Mrs. Newman. She placed her boot firmly across mine and pressed down hard.

The secretary, a Miss Patty Primley, according to the nameplate on her desk, cleared her throat.

"Mother's name?" she whispered.

"Madame Caterina." Another pause.

"Occupation?"

"Clairvoyant." I smiled sweetly, as if I'd said, "Clerk at Murray's Hardware."

Mrs. Newman stepped in. "Perhaps I could accompany Annie to her classroom, Miss Primley, so that she doesn't miss more than necessary. If you could stamp her entry pass, I'll come back to fill in any missing information on the long form."

Entering room 305, while class was in progress, was one of the bravest things I'd ever done. Mrs. Newman watched from the door for a moment, as if to remind me of my duty to stay put.

The class fell silent as I came in. The teacher, Mr. Fanshawe, stood by the chalkboard straight ahead of me, with a sea, really, a shimmering sea of faces off to my left. I did not dare to turn my head. My fingers, gripping the entry pass, began to cramp.

Mr. Fanshawe had been tapping the chalkboard with the tip of a pointer. He looked at me, head cocked to one side, and reached out for my pass without lowering his other arm or losing his place.

"Hold this," he said, indicating that we should do a trade. I was to take the pointer while he examined my pass. Could you die? said the voice in my brain.

I kept my back to the class, my face now blazing like the morning sun, examining rectangles on the chalkboard labeled ANTECHAMBER, and ANNEX, and BURIAL CHAMBER.

"Ladies and gentlemen," said Mr. Fanshawe, "this is Miss

Annie Grackle. Miss Grackle, sit down there in the second row. Clive Morrison is absent today. We'll find you a desk of your own tomorrow. See me later for catch-up work."

He took back the pointer without noticing my catatonic condition. I was forced to turn around and move to my place.

I saw where Sammy Sloane was sitting, two rows over from Clive's desk and two rows back. Smack in front of Clive's desk was Delia de Groot. There were other familiar faces swimming to the surface, but I sat down, faced forward and listened hard.

"Well, Miss Grackle," said Mr. Fanshawe. "The topic under discussion is the religious beliefs of the ancient world. In particular, we are looking at the death practices in Egypt and Mesopotamia, greatly enlightened by the recent discovery of a royal pharoah's tomb, the tomb of the boy king Tutankhamen. Are you following me?"

Did he mean me to speak out loud?

"Yes, sir," I croaked. To prove it, I added, "Dead king in Egypt."

Someone behind me snickered, but the teacher ignored it.

"Who would like to tell Miss Grackle what was uncovered in that tomb?"

Several hands went up. Not that I looked around, but I could feel the air shifting.

"Miss Carlaw?"

Ah, the popular Sally, somewhere close to the window.

"A mummy, sir. The king, all wrapped in linen, embalmed in perfume, inside a golden coffin."

"Very good. Anyone else? Miss Blaine?"

"Treasure, sir. A throne, and golden boats."

"Yes. Anyone else? Mr. Pittsfield?"

The boy I knew as Pitts had been waving his fingers almost up Mr. Fanshawe's nose.

"Food in jars, sir. And dead cats. And the king's internal organs in another jar."

There was laughter all around me.

"And what was all this for? Mr. Sloane?"

I caught my breath and turned without thinking to look at Sammy. He saw me, hesitated and then blushed. Oh, that blush thrilled me to the soles of my feet. I heard a noise in Delia's throat and knew she'd seen it too.

"Uh, it was all for the afterlife, sir. They thought they would need supplies in Heaven, except they called it the Kingdom of the West. I believe they went there, all right, but as spirits, without bodies. They wouldn't need all that jewelry and junk, so it just stayed in the tomb."

"Thank you, Mr. Sloane. Do you understand all this, Miss Grackle?"

I was tugged back to attention. "Yes, sir."

"Do you have anything to contribute on the subject of an afterlife?"

"I hope I die with a clear conscience," I said, after a moment. "It's the spirits with regrets who have an agitated afterlife. Though naturally, most of them regret being dead."

I saw Sammy laughing, and heard everyone else.

"An important point, Miss Grackle," said Mr. Fanshawe. "Please consider the question, tenth grade: Did the Egyptians look forward to death?" He glanced at the clock above the doorway. "We'll have to pursue this next lesson. The history reading for tonight is chapter nine, beginning on page sixty-four of your text. Miss Grackle, come to me at the end of the day for a textbook and missing assignments. Prepare now for Miss Croft."

A bell trilled in the hallway, formally announcing Miss Croft's arrival, as Mr. Fanshawe left the room. Quiet groans greeted a tall woman, skinny as a green bean. Mathematics, I guessed, and I was right.

"Display your work, ladies and gentlemen."

While books thumped and desk lids banged, Delia turned around to hiss at me.

"Can't you see how embarrassing it is for Sammy Sloane when you stare at him all the time?"

Ouch! She might as well have scratched my face with her fingernails. I blinked to hold back instant tears.

Was it true? Did Sammy cringe when he thought of me? Or was Delia only jealous and purposely slicing me up into little bits? How would I ever learn all the secrets of high school?

12

If you drop a knife,
you will receive a male visitor.

As if I hadn't had enough of Delia, I met her father the same afternoon. Or at least, I witnessed my mother meeting him. I already knew who he was, of course. A person couldn't live in Peach Hill and not notice the police force. Officer de Groot was tall and wide and hairy. Officer Rankin was the short one I'd seen outside Carlaw's the day I left first grade. He was slight, with a surprisingly deep voice and a face like a stoat. The yardage in blue serge required to sew Delia's father's uniform must have been twice that for his fellow constable. They'd been nicknamed de Gorilla and de Runt long before Mama and I set foot on Needle Street.

I trudged home from school, lugging my new textbooks, kicking leaves and miserably dreaming up clever retorts to spit in Delia's face. I'd forced all thoughts of Sammy into a dark brain crevice. From the corner of Needle Street I saw a line outside our doorway of more than a dozen women awaiting an audience with Madame Caterina.

Silly geese. If only they knew she mocked them with

every false promise they bought from her. What would they think if they knew she'd sent her own daughter off to school without so much as a wave that morning? Would they be lining up to listen to her nonsense? Humph. But they didn't know, couldn't know, would never know.

All I wanted was a wedge of Peg's pie. I backed up and stomped along the alley behind the house to come in through the kitchen.

The door to the front room was closed. Mama had one of the ladies in with her. Peg was gone early, but she'd left a lemon pie on the table to celebrate my first day of high school. Someone knocked on the front door. The knife slipped from my fingers and skittered across the tiles. I heard Mama and her client in the hall.

"Good," I muttered, picking up the knife. "Let her answer her own door." I put a slice of pie on a plate and balanced it on top of my books for the journey to my bedroom.

"Do come back for another session, Miss Chambers. I'm certain we can reduce the size of those warts and contact your sister again. One dollar, please." The door was opened as Miss Chambers chirruped, "Good-bye."

Mama said, "Why, Officer! Hello!" Her voice told me she was not pleased. "What an unexpected pleasure!"

Boots shuffled on the wooden floor. "Ma'am," said a man's voice. I put down my books and pie and sat on the floor next to them, in the alcove outside the kitchen.

"Would you care to come in for a cup of—"

What would she offer this hefty lout? If it hadn't been for alcohol being outlawed throughout the country, I'd have guessed he was a whiskey-drinking man.

"A cup of peppermint tea, perhaps? Or a shot of Wilky's Silk Elixir?" She said the word "elixir" as if it were the naughtiest suggestion she could come up with. I could feel the heat of his blush all the way down the hall.

"Oh, no. No, ma'am, thank you, no, ma'am."

His boots clicked about on the hard floor, and he couldn't keep his voice steady even for a sentence.

"I'm here on duty, ma'am." He got ahold of himself. "There are loiterers outside your door, ma'am. We're a quiet town, ma'am. We can't have all this fuss in the street."

"I'm not sure what you might have heard about us, Officer. Do you know of the miracle that has healed my daughter? After a lifetime of my Annie's affliction, I've been blessed with the gift to cure her. You, with a daughter of your own, you, especially, must know how I feel." She let that one sink in. Most people fell for the "you, especially" technique.

Mama must have been studying my notes. That was why I was listening to this performance. I'd become allergic to policemen after Carling. The soles of my feet started itching to run, and my eyes squeezed shut to block out the scenery. But Mama, a true professional, calmly followed her own motto: "There is no one more useful as a friend than a police constable."

And no one more dangerous as an enemy. Except, as I would find out, a police constable's daughter.

"My own hands have given me the gift I prayed for," purred Mama. "My little girl has shaken off the troubled shadows. It's only natural that people should line up for a share of the healing."

"I can understand that, ma'am. I'm right happy for you. But it's disturbing the quiet of the neighborhood. Do they all have to be here at the same time, crowding up the public street?"

"Officer de Groot . . ." Mama paused. "Am I right? It is Officer de Groot?"

"Montgomery de Groot, ma'am. At your service."

"Montgomery? That *is* a fine big name."

Suitable for a large, fleshy, red-faced bear like yourself, she managed not to say.

"Monty, ma'am, really. My wife, well, the fellows, well, mostly I'm called Monty."

"Monty, then. The thing about a lineup . . ." Her voice dropped to a confidential whisper. "A lineup is good for business! A woman goes to market in the morning, thinking of nothing but the choice she has to make between chops and chicken. She sees a cluster of other women, each of them yearning for the answer to a dream, and *poof!* The struggles of the day disappear and her own dreams are kindled. I can answer some of life's most difficult questions, Monty. I can change the way you face your days."

I knew her hand was resting on the sleeve of his uniform. I could just feel it. I knew her eyes were shining up into his. "And perhaps," she whispered, "help you sleep a little better at night."

Ew. She had no shame. First Mr. Poole and now the policeman. The men of Peach Hill were falling like ninepins. Why did it work so well? Were men just so dull-witted and vain that pretty words made them dance like puppets? And why did Mama want puppets, anyway? She should find someone who was funny and handsome, like Sammy Sloane, and live in a cottage with a veranda.

But she did have the memory of an elephant. It was weeks before that I'd told her the police constable's wife had run off last spring, coincidentally on the same day the fish man came through with fresh halibut. Estelle de Groot had taken only one dress and a change of lingerie, according to Mrs. Ford and the other loyal wives squeezing tomatoes at Carlaw's. All the ladies seemed more envious than scandalized. At school, Delia claimed that her mother was dead. Better than admitting the shameful truth, I supposed, though maybe she wouldn't see it as shameful if she knew for sure that her mother was happy.

Officer de Groot coughed and I heard the boots shuffle again. "I was only suggesting you make appointments with them, ma'am."

"Call me Caterina."

"Yes, ma'am. Thank you. I'd better be off. It was just to tell you to limit the commotion."

I peered around the corner to watch the finale. They wouldn't notice me now. Officer de Groot, not knowing how to make his exit, put out a paw as if to shake on a business deal.

Mama grasped it with both her hands and turned it over. There was barely enough light to find the doorknob, so I knew she was bluffing when she said, "Oh, my!" in that fluttering way. "Oh, Monty! You have a fascinating arrangement of lines on your palm. I would be most intrigued to examine them closely. Would you like to come back this evening? On your way home from the station? Free of charge, of course. The pleasure will be all mine."

"That would be—uh—I would like that very much. But, uh, not till Tuesday. I'm on late duty till next Tuesday."

"Till Tuesday, then," said Mama. She released his hand and he groped for the handle of the door. If he were smart, he would never step into our hallway again. But he clearly was not smart.

As the door closed behind him, Mama spun around and pointed a finger at me. "I don't like you spying on me," she said, "but I hope you took note that friendliness to men in uniform is an important skill and one you should be learning."

"Why didn't it work in Carling?" I dared to ask.

Mama flinched. "Because the uniform in Carling was stretched to cover three at once," she said. "The sheriff, his wife and God. Now, get out there"—she pointed toward Needle Street—"and pick one who looks likely."

"Looks likely" was Mama's way of saying good shoes, real bird feathers on the hat, jeweled watch, bulge in pocketbook . . .

I brought in a lady in a sealskin jacket and set up appointment times for everyone else to come back.

Stooping down to collect my stack of schoolbooks, I had a sudden thought. Who was Mama, really?

How did I know if Mama told the truth about anything? Just because she said something different to me from what she said to the rest of the world, did that make it true? Or was it just a different falsehood? What did I know about anything, except what Mama had taught me? Did that mean I was really as ignorant as an idiot?

My slice of pie sat untouched on its plate.

13

A uniformed person in your dream foretells that a wealthy person will come to your aid.

My first several days of high school made me hot and cold, made me crow and cry and cringe. Each day held thunderclaps of embarrassment and sprinklings of delight. I never knew in the morning how supper would find me, other than worn to threads from being so alert. And keeping my chin up, no matter what comments Mama tossed my way. She couldn't stop herself, maybe guessing that the more I went to school, the more I would realize there were things my mother was wrong about.

I hadn't expected the lessons to be interesting. Some of the teachers were dull, of course, but even that was worth considering. Shouldn't a classroom be a theater, with the students enthralled? Why did Mr. Goldin use the deadliest drone to describe the violent exploitation of Congo natives? Why did Mrs. Baker choose poems about willow trees and raindrops, when there were others in the same book about highwaymen? These puzzles and many more were my entertainment each day, for now I had a mission. I would discover, for myself, what lay beyond my mother's doorstep: a universe of knowledge and truth and the mysteries of friendship.

"It is most gratifying to finally have an eager scholar," Miss Croft would say, causing an epidemic of spinning eyeballs. I'd never had much to do with numbers beyond counting dollar bills and converting them at the bank into twenties, but it turned out that I was a natural at mathematics.

"Miss Grackle has achieved another perfect score."

A muttered chorus of "Goody-goody toady girl" burned my ears. Which was better, pride in my cleverness or winning friends? It seemed easier, by far, to please the teachers than my classmates.

Girls kept me at a distance. I caught Sammy looking my way a few times, but if ever he seemed about to approach, up popped Sally or Delia or some other distraction.

I found my place for eating lunch. There was a tree near the gate, too far from the benches or the ball field to be a place for the others to congregate. I found a spot, between two huge roots, that fit my bottom exactly and had a good view of the yard and the street. With that mighty trunk at my back, no one could sneak up on me. I kept an eye on Delia's crowd and on Sammy's gleaming hair.

At noon one day, I spied the pansies on Mrs. Newman's hat bobbing toward the schoolyard. She was dragging the girl from the alley with a death grip on her wrist. The girl's bare feet stubbornly slowed progress every step of the way.

Mrs. Newman's mouth was set in a grim, triumphant line

as she moved her iron claw to the girl's shoulder and marched her through the gate. I wondered where the sneaky old bat had managed to catch her, since I'd had no luck myself. It must have been in a very tight corner, with no chance for the girl to dart away like a swift little cockroach. I couldn't picture Mrs. Newman lurking about in the alley behind the bakery.

I felt pity at the girl's plight more than at my own. I was just contrary; she was downright untamed. For me, school had become a sanctuary away from home and the world of Madame Caterina. But would the alley girl ever show up without an escort? Would Mrs. Newman need to provide this service every morning?

They stopped at the school steps. From my spot beside the tree, I could not hear, but I could see Mrs. Newman pointing and the girl scowling as she sat down on the step and pretended to brush off the soles of her feet.

The wide front door swung open just then, and Miss Primley came out, grasping the big brass yard bell. She rang it ten times, arm swinging in an arc, front to back, alerting everyone from here to Wyoming that the lunch recess was over.

The hubbub of students lining up blocked my view for a few minutes, but as the crowd filed inside, I saw Mrs. Newman take off her shoes, low pumps dyed the color of periwinkles. She put them on the ground in front of the girl while Miss Primley waved her hands about, probably objecting. Mrs. Newman just stood there in stockinged feet, nodding at the girl. The ground must have felt cold through her stockings, and the silk would be shredded in no time with the pebbles and twigs strewn everywhere. Mrs. Newman didn't shift or shuffle.

The girl pulled on the pumps. They were too big, but she stroked the leather with her dirty fingertips. Miss Primley clapped her hands and the girl jumped, *clomp-clomp*ing up the steps. The secretary ushered her inside but turned with a final gesture; she rotated her finger next to her temple, the way a kid would say "you're crazy."

Mrs. Newman just smiled and waved good-bye. She tiptoed to the gate and paused under the tree, three feet from where I hid. She lifted her skirt, unhooked her garters, rolled down her stockings and slipped them off. She scrunched them into a ball and put them into her pocketbook. She gave away her fancy shoes and walked home barefoot! What kind of woman believed that going to school was so important? I watched until she was well down the street before I raced for the GIRLS door, late for biology class.

I didn't see the girl from the alley again that day, but I heard from the yammer amongst the students that she'd been placed in the ninth grade.

And sure enough, Delia's father came back that evening. Mama and I had done our research, going over the charts and notes for every scrap she might use. I sneaked into my corner while Mama primped in front of her mirror. This was one show I did not mean to miss, better than a story on the radio.

Mama sat Officer de Groot down in the red armchair. It creaked under his weight, and I had a vision of the carved legs splintering with a loud snap and him crashing, *whomp*, to the floor amidst the debris, with his enormous shiny boots stuck straight out in front and a look of astonishment on his face. And me, exposed for the nosy spy that I was, squished beneath the broken velvet chunks of chair.

"This will be a new experience for you," Mama was saying, her voice soothing as a lozenge. "But you must try to leave your reservations outside the door. In here, it's just you and me, no walls and no secrets. Did you know that the word 'clairvoyant' means 'seeing clearly'? I cannot see clearly if you stand guard against me, can I?"

I suppose he shook his head.

"That's right. Now, let me warm your hands to stimulate the connection between your heart and your heart's path, to energize your aura and prepare your soul to share with me." Sometimes I shook my head in wonder, listening to my mother spout nonsense.

There were a few quiet moments while my mother adjusted the light and no doubt cradled his hand in her own. I couldn't hear him breathing and worried that he might pass out from holding his breath in.

"I see conflict under your roof," said Mama, which she often said to begin, because what roof is not harboring conflict of some sort? On the rare occasion when the customer said, "Conflict? I live alone. There's no conflict," Mama had an answer for that, too: "Ah, but there will be soon, for I see turbulence in your forecast." Or something along those lines.

But with Officer de Groot, her opening suggestion was enough.

"You see conflict? My hand tells you that?"

"That and much more," she murmured. "I also see two beautiful women."

"My daughter," he said. "And, I suppose, my wife. But she is no longer with us."

"Ah," said Mama. "But not yet of the spirit world?"

"She left," he whispered.

"Ah," said Mama. "There was conflict, as I suggested."

"She didn't like being a policeman's wife," he admitted. "She moved away."

"But not alone?"

"How—?"

"Your palm," explained Mama, "shows a betrayal. But I can see that you were true of heart and not the deceiver."

"Well," said Officer de Groot, whispering. "She went off with another fellow, but it's not public knowledge."

Oh, yes it is, I thought. All over the square.

"And your daughter?" prodded Mama. "There is trouble with your daughter?"

"She pretends that Estelle is dead," he said. "The shame is too great for her to bear. But she's her mother's daughter, she's sassy and often disobedient." He coughed. "I really, this is not, I shouldn't . . ." The chair creaked with his uneasiness.

"Please!" said Mama. "It is my profession to honor your secrets. Discretion is essential to trust. You trust me, don't you? As you couldn't trust your wife?"

Ew.

"Let me look at the rest of your lines," she said quickly. "See here? Your life line? You have a long life ahead, Officer—"

"Call me Monty."

"A long life, Monty. I see tribulation along the way, but you will find peace."

As if that fortune would not suit anyone who ventured through the door!

"I will?"

"You will. And speaking of finding things, you might like to know that my abilities as a medium are quite renowned. I could track down your wife, if you wish."

"Really?"

"Though naturally the cost of psychic discovery is quite high."

"Well, I'll think about it, ma'am. I'm not sure there'd be any point." He stood up. I plugged my ears, hard, so I wouldn't have to hear the way she said good-bye to him. Some things really were too painful for a delicate girl like me.

14

If you do not present a new pair of shoes to a poor person at least once during your life, you will go barefoot in the next world.

"Do we have any clothing we no longer use?" I asked Mama. "I'm collecting for the needy."

"You're what? The who?"

"The needy, Mama. Poor people who do not have enough clothing to wear."

"Nonsense," said Mama.

"There is a girl at school who has no shoes," I told her. "And I'm sure she's not the only one. So I thought I'd collect outgrown clothes and take them as a gift."

Mama shook her head. "You amaze me," she said. "I've raised a missionary. However did that happen? You'll be sailing away to Africa before I know it." She dealt another row of tarot cards and examined them closely.

"So, do we?" I insisted. "Have extra clothes?"

"Only if you've grown too fat to fit them," Mama said.

"I can decide?" I asked. "It's up to me?"

"You're only depriving yourself." She didn't look up from the Empress card.

"I'm collecting clothing for the needy," I told Peg. "Do you have anything you'd like to contribute?"

"Honey," she said, "I am the needy."

I'd never thought about that before. Here was Peg, working for us and then going home to work some more for her ungrateful father.

"Why don't you have a husband, Peg?"

"Just don't have one *yet*," she said. "I aim to find one, but none of the scaredy-cat men I've met want anything to do with me as long as my father lives and breathes. I'm going to have to poison his tea before I get a beau."

"That's what I think about Mama," I said. "And not just boys, any friend at all. She jolts the bejeebies out of anyone who ever meets her, except in the front room."

"She's scary, all right," muttered Peg, giving a careful look at the doorway first.

"But anyway," I said. "There's this needy person I've noticed, and I want to give her some things."

"Who is she?" asked Peg. "I probably know her."

I hesitated. I couldn't think of a reason not to tell her, though often the reason didn't show up until after the telling was done. But maybe Peg would know where she lived.

"It's this girl," I said. "She's a bit younger than me, and smaller. She wears raggedy overalls and looks a bit rough."

"Dark hair?" asked Peg. "Big, moony eyes and dirty hands?"

"Uh-huh."

"That's the Wilky girl. I'm surprised you had a reason to meet her. She's not at the school, is she?"

"How do you know that?"

"Reverend Wilky and his wife, Tabitha, who was Tabitha Crane before she married that man, they don't believe in school. They believe children will learn what they need to know through the guidance of a heavenly hand. So far, that hand seems to be leading their own child into nothing but trouble."

"What kind of trouble?"

Peg looked at me and ruffled my hair just like back when I was a moron. "Nothing you need to know about, honey. It's a nice impulse, you thinking you could help that girl, but she is beyond help. Certainly any kind you could give her. Reverend Wilky has the kind of opinions a team of oxen couldn't shift."

"Does he have a church?"

"If you can call it a church. He's got what used to be a living room in the front of his house out on the Way. Now it's full of every kind of broken-down, rubbishy chair and bench that he could salvage from anyone's back door all over town. He has his wife and child dragging furniture and anything else from wherever they find it. He's got about twenty regulars, I'd say. They squeeze in there on a Sunday morning and listen to the Reverend stomp his feet and thump his chest and squeeze the Word of God out of thin air.

"He makes a tonic that he sells as a sideline: Wilky's Silk Revitalizing Elixir. That stuff just flies out of there on Sundays, not to mention Saturday nights. Between you and me and the bedpost, that stuff should be called Wilky's Kick-in-the-Pants instead of Silk. It's like drinking gasoline."

"How do you know so much about it?" I asked.

"I went there once."

"You did?"

"I was curious, that's all. A girl from my own church, St. Alphonse, switched over and started going there. But I knew after ten minutes it wasn't for me."

"Why not?"

"I like to worship in a place that smells good, not like boiled carrots, and where the pews are hard and smooth and holy. I like when the priest talks in that fancy language that I don't understand, makes me feel he's closer to God. Reverend Wilky, well, he just scares me. Tells folks they're sinners and have to pay for a chance to see the heavenly gates. What's the point in trying down here if it won't take you someplace better?"

"I still think his daughter deserves to have shoes," I said. "Mrs. Newman gave the girl her shoes just so she could go to school."

"Her name is Helen," said Peg. "She probably sold the shoes the next day to pay for a week's worth of macaroni. Don't think I'm hardhearted, Annie. I've spent some time feeling sorry for that girl, but after she took my Sunday slip right off the line, along with six pairs of my father's socks? That's where my sorry goes straight out to the ashcan. Even if her father put the socks on and thanked her for them, even if he sent her out to get them! There has to be a point where a child is smart enough to know right from wrong, and stands up in the face of it."

I stopped thinking about Helen right there and started thinking about myself. Peg had accidentally poked a stick into a tender spot. Was I smart enough to know right from wrong? Was I going to stand up and do something about it?

I found a pair of shoes that no longer fit me, and an old tunic the color of mulberries that I'd never liked anyway. From the costume trunk, I pilfered a green jacket and a couple of chiffon scarves. Not the essentials, but at least Helen would have her own shoes. I made a bundle and set it beside my bedroom door. Delivery would be another challenge.

One morning, without even meaning to, I stepped outside at the very moment when Sammy was passing by. His smile erased the hundred hours of wishing for it.

"You've been avoiding me," he said.

"No," I said, glancing around for Delia.

"You act so shy," said Sammy, "but you're not really."

"Why do you say that?"

"You must be friendly to be in contact with other worlds," he said. "Like an ambassador."

I had a choice. I could tell him flat out that I knew little enough of this world, let alone any other, or I could continue to feel warm all over, under his sunny gaze.

"It's really my mother who travels to the Great Beyond," I said. "But I'm learning."

"I bet you're really good at it," said Sammy. He stopped walking and looked straight at me. I looked straight back at him, my heart thrashing under Mama's cashmere cardigan.

"Hello, Sammy Sloane!" Giggles showered us on all sides.

They came from the girl named Lexie and two of her ninth-grade friends.

"Hello, Lexie," said Sammy. "Do you know Annie? Annie, this is Lexie and Ruthie and Jean."

"Hello," I said, as if I hadn't eavesdropped on their conversations a dozen times. We were nearly at the school gate.

"You're the one who used to be, uh, poorly, aren't you?" said Jean, peering though smudged eyeglasses.

Jean:
Likes to eat popped corn with maple syrup.
Hates spiders.

"That's one way of putting it," I said.

"I heard you were an idiot," said Ruthie, who was round and pink.

Ruthie:
Cried for a week when her turtle crossed over.
Not allowed to wear lipstick.

"She's got the Gift," said Sammy, as proud as if he'd given it to me himself. "She can see into the future and talk to spirits."

"Is that true?" asked Jean, squinting.

"Can you really?" said Lexie.

I felt Sammy's eyes on me and succumbed instantly to temptation. "Well, yes," I admitted. "Since I was healed, I have entered a trance and received messages from a girl who died in the thirteenth century."

Miss Primley's bell clanged from the steps.

"What?" said Lexie.

"You have?" exclaimed Sammy. "I'll have to hear about that!"

The bell kept going. Sammy headed toward the BOYS door, and I followed the girls to our entrance.

"What does that mean?" asked Jean. "How can you receive messages from someone who's dead?"

"I go into a trance and the spirit takes me over. She uses me to write her words down on paper." It sounded dumb now that Sammy was gone.

"Will you show us?"

"Well, it doesn't just happen," I said. "There are preparations and circumstances . . ."

"Will you eat lunch with us?" invited Lexie. "We've noticed that you're always alone. Do you want to sit with us today?"

As silly as it seemed, I thought just possibly I'd hear the secret of being a regular girl. So I ate lunch with them, sitting on a bench near the water fountain instead of nestled between the roots of my tree.

One thing I learned was that I was not the only girl to have noticed the charms of Sammy Sloane.

"Ooooh! He's so cute!" said Jean.

"He makes me quiver all over!" moaned Ruthie.

"If he could stop talking about Sherlock Holmes for five minutes," said Lexie. "I'll take Terence Price any day."

Sammy Sloane, Freddy Blau and Terence Price, those were the three. And the girls started to chant: "*Sammy*

Sloane? Mine alone! Freddy Blau? And how! Terence Price? Kiss me twice!" And then they collapsed with hysterical laughter. Well, I thought Freddy was conceited, and Terence Price had hair that hung about his ears like oiled thread. I'd put Sammy far above the others, but my only hope of being his choice was my dubious connection to the Other Side. So was it me he'd be choosing, or my mother's daughter?

"Mama," I said as Peg and I set the table for supper. "I've been invited to spend the night in the home of one of my new school friends."

I counted silently to ten. Mama watched me, perhaps waiting for me to say I was joking.

"On Saturday night," I said. "I've told Lexie I'd like to come. It's a sleeping-over party, with two other girls."

No reply.

"She lives on Walnut Street, in one of those big houses."

No reply.

"Mama. Say something."

"This is not wise, Annie." She had to be careful, with Peg right there listening as she folded the napkins. That was why I'd chosen that moment.

"It decreases our mystical appeal if we appear ordinary in any context."

"Please, Mama? Please? I want to be ordinary."

"No, you do not. I don't want to hear you say that ever again."

"I'm sorry, I don't mean ordinary, I mean . . ."

What could I tell her? I meant ordinary. I meant not unusual, not a freak, unremarkable, not remarked upon, not weird—ordinary. For the occasional Saturday night, anyway.

"I mean—I want to have friends," I said.

"You don't need friends," sniffed Mama. I looked at Peg.

"Lexie Johns?" said Peg, trying to help. "She's a nice girl. Her daddy owns the lumber mill by the river."

"That's the one," I said, feeling Mama's breathing quicken next to me. "Ruthie said that Lexie has a big bedroom with two canopy beds, just for overnight guests."

"Her mother belongs to the country club over in Timmons," said Peg. "One of the first women ever to play golf there. She goes out every Saturday. I know the girl, Alice, who's the maid over there. Says Mrs. Johns just throws out her golf shoes if the course was muddy and buys a new pair. Alice never has to clean them."

Peg went to stir butter into the rice.

"You keep your ears open" was all Mama said to me after that.

15

It is bad luck to point at the moon.

I packed my suitcase with a bubble of glee rising in my throat. Don't be too excited, I warned myself; these are silly girls. But I was eager to study the ceremonies of friendship close up.

I wished I had a new nightdress instead of old flannel pajamas from the boys' department at the F. W. Woolworth Co. in Hawley. I slipped into Mama's room and rifled her drawers.

Almost at once I uncovered a stash of paper money, rolled in bundles an inch thick and tied with narrow blue ribbon. All our customers paid in cash, of course, to hear their futures told. Like a squirrel who hides nuts in more than one tree, Mama kept her money in several secret places. She knew there were occasions when a speedy departure could not wait for banking hours. There were eight bundles here in the drawer, and more in the muslin sugar sack in the pantry, and in a hatbox on the shelf in the hall closet, and lying in the false bottom of our trunk. Each bundle held twenty

twenty-dollar bills. Four hundred dollars, multiplied by how many bundles altogether? A lot of money. Enough to buy a house?

But I was not looking for money at the moment.

I touched the silk pouches that held Mama's necklaces and rings, and two photographs in gilded leather frames. One was of me, when I was five years old, sitting on the step of our Lenny's Famous caravan, wearing the biggest hair bow you ever saw. The other picture was slightly out of focus, and though I'd never told Mama I'd seen it, let alone had her show it to me, I liked to think it was my father.

Mama said my father had died in the Great War, but I didn't believe her. I thought she didn't know where my father was and didn't like to admit it. She'd made up a good story over the years, but I'd been paying attention and the details changed quite a bit from telling to telling.

I was pretty sure his name was William because usually she referred to him as Will, except the once when he was Henry. Where they met was either at a dance or at a party at a friend's house, or one time she said a museum in New York City. They might have been married or they might not, but I suspected not.

"Was his name William Grey?" I'd asked, and she'd laughed before realizing I might really care to know. And then she said, "No, no, it wasn't. I used my maiden name professionally and it was best to keep it that way."

Whoever he was, he was gone now.

I found a silk shift, never worn in my company, folded in tissue paper beneath Mama's personal garments. Oh, it was lovely, the way it rippled over my fingers almost like water. I rolled it into the bottom of my suitcase, with a change of underclothing and a fresh blouse. I put in my hairbrush and my toothbrush. What else? I wanted my suitcase to be full to the brim. It seemed like a momentous expedition—as if I were making a journey as far as the Pacific Ocean or the Baltic Sea. But I was only going to Lexie's house, so I shut the lid and snapped closed the catches. No one had to know it was my first night away from the home of my mother, aside from those grim hours on a cot at the sheriff's house in Carling. No one except my mother knew about that.

My stomach was in knots during supper. I moved the food around, spread out the peas, chopped up the chicken into tiny pieces. I didn't want Mama using a poor appetite as an excuse to cancel the evening. Peg stayed to tidy and then handed me a waxed-paper packet.

"I made some raspberry jumbles for your little party tonight," she said. "A surefire path to popularity is to arrive with raspberry jumbles."

"Oh, thank you, Peg!" I clasped her in my arms and kissed her on the cheek. "How would I know anything without you?"

I heard Mama snort but chose to ignore her. I looked at her only once more, when I waved from the door and stepped out into the navy blue night.

As Peg had said, Lexie lived in one of the "grand houses" of Peach Hill, one street over from Mr. Poole's. The wide front porch overlooked a front lawn nearly the size of the town square. The other girls were there already, all piled into a porch swing that hung from the rafters like a cradle. It creaked and groaned under the weight of three giggling, writhing bodies. The handle of my suitcase got slippery, I was clutching it so tightly. At last their giddiness faded and they noticed that I was there.

"You've come!"

"Come in, we've been waiting!"

"Annie's here!"

The swing squawked as they all jumped off.

"Come in, come in, we've had the best idea!" They dragged me inside, where Lexie's mother appeared, summoned by the noise. She was wearing a soft blue suit and had her hair bobbed, like a lady in a magazine.

"Hello, darlings!"

Lexie kissed her mother and clasped her hand.

"Hello, Mummy. This is Annie. Remember? I told you?"

The weight of that "told" swung like an ominous tree branch above my head. "Told" meant all the rumors, all the dirt: "I'm bringing home the town oddball, be polite!"

"Ah, yes! Annie! How nice that you could come tonight."

"Good evening, Mrs. Johns," I said.

"I'll send Alice up shortly with snacks for you girls."

"I brought raspberry jumbles."

"Oohh!" squeaked the girls.

"Why, Annie, that's lovely of you. Would you all like lemonade to go with your treats?"

Her niceness made me dizzy.

I was hauled up the stairs, into Lexie's bedroom. They spun me around so I could see the enormous princess beds with gauzy canopies, the thick rug, the flounced curtains, the vanity table lit up on both sides of the mirror with twinkling lights.

"Look what Lexie has!" Ruthie thrust something at me.

"It's a Ouija board!" they cried, bubbling over. "Everybody has one now!"

"And we thought—" said Lexie.

"We thought," said Ruthie, "since you have a natural ability—"

"—you could probably summon the dead," said Jean, "or contact that spirit girl you mentioned and—"

"—bring her ghost here! To my bedroom!"

What could I do? This was exactly what my mother had feared, that silly girls all over the country were joining the craze for spirit calling and would stop paying the professionals. But silly girls couldn't do it right. Only clever ones could.

"Have you seen a Ouija board before?" asked Lexie when I hesitated.

"Uh, yes. Yes, of course," I said. "I was only thinking. To do this properly, we should make some preparations."

More squeals and clapping hands and jumping up and down.

"Do you have any candles?"

"I wouldn't be allowed candles in my bedroom," said Lexie.

Jean and Ruthie pouted. "Come on, Lexie, can't you sneak them?"

"We don't need them," I said quickly, seeing Lexie's doubt. "Look, there's a moon. It'll be high enough in no time. We'll use that." I pulled apart the frothy curtains. Lexie turned off the row of lights above her vanity and the lamp in the ceiling. Moonlight trickled across the floor and Lexie's bed in a weak stripe. The darker the better, for my purposes.

"My mother always says the moon draws out secrets," I said, making up my patter on the spot. "The same way it rules the tides."

"Ooh."

"What's it like to have your mother?" asked Jean.

"She's the only one I have, so it's normal to me."

"She's very pretty," said Ruthie, as if she were handing me a present.

"Yes. Thank you."

"Do you think she'll get married again?" asked Jean. "My parents saw her driving out with Mr. Poole. Father was saying a fellow couldn't be blamed for going into debt over a filly like that."

"Jean!"

"I'm only saying what my father said."

"Couldn't your mother go into a trance and find out if she's going to fall in love?" asked Lexie.

"Ooh, think of that!" cried Ruthie. "Does she have a crystal ball?"

How did I get myself here? I wondered. What pathetic, lonely part of me thought this would be fun?

"A clairvoyant doesn't necessarily see what will happen," I explained. "She is sensitive to likelihood. She sees what probably will happen."

"Oh."

"But seeing into the future is quite different from talking to a spirit who has passed to the Other Side," I said.

"Let's try the Ouija board," said Ruthie.

"We have paper," said Jean. "In case your ghost girl shows up."

"Good idea," I said. "May we sit on your bed, Lexie? And put the Ouija board directly in the moonlight? That will rouse the spirits and make them more receptive."

"Ooh!"

They scrambled to remove their shoes, as did I, since that was the point of the suggestion. We settled more or less in a circle on the billowy eiderdown. I tucked my left foot—always the best cracker—neatly under the Ouija board, which rested on our knees.

I showed them how to place their fingers lightly on the planchette so that it could move easily from letter to letter while the spirits spelled out answers.

"Let's take turns asking," said Lexie. "Me first because it's my Ouija board." No one could argue with that.

"Oh, Great Ouija!" Lexie intoned. "Come to us and share your wisdom! Come unto us, O spirit!"

I cracked my toe.

The girls screamed loudly enough to break glass. It was a wonder Lexie's mother didn't rush in with bandages.

"The spirit is here!" I whispered. "What do you want to know?"

"Will Terence Price invite me to the Christmas dance?" asked Lexie.

For cat's sake! I thought. The planchette slid to YES, obviously guided by three eager spiritualists.

"Yes! Ouija said yes!"

This was too dumb. Time to jazz things up. I uttered a terrified moan and went rigid, with my legs jerking into stiff rods. I tipped the board over while my head flipped back and my chest arched forward.

"Hey! What are you doing?" The girls bounced out of the way of my kicking feet.

"What's wrong with her? Oh my God, she's having a seizure!"

"Get your mother, Lexie, this is scary!"

"No," said Lexie, "I think it's the spirit she told us about."

"Give her the paper!"

"Find a pencil!"

"OhmygoodnessgraciousMarymotherofGod!"

The girls jabbered like ninnies.

I kept twitching and whimpering like an ailing goat.

Lexie put a pencil in my hand and adjusted the Ouija board so that I could use it as a desk. I could hardly see in the dark, but I began to scrawl while they leaned over me, as entranced as if I were the reincarnation of William Shakespeare.

My name is Gwendalen of Stone House, I wrote. *I am daughter to Arne the Vast and Elbecca of Tune. I have found a willing vessel in the form of Annie Grackle and in this way must tell my tale.*

"What is she doing?" asked Ruthie in a whisper.

"She's been possessed," hissed Lexie.

"Is this a sin?" asked Jean.

"Shhh."

My father tried to have me wed more times than I can count, but the price was always higher than he cared to pay. He preferred to keep me out of sight during all encounters with the prospective bridegrooms. I confess that I was not a lovely maid. I have a wide,

117

turned-up nose. My brothers called me Piggy. The dowry could never be high enough.

"Oh, how sad," whispered Jean. Lexie pushed a new sheet of paper under my pencil.

My family's wish to have me gone from home was understandable. The nuns of Saint Lucy's welcomed me, realizing I would have no place in the world other than what they offered me. They were not to know how brief my time with them would be.

My hand was getting tired. I paused to give it a shake.

"How did you die?" asked Jean.

My father discovered that I had—what was that word? Ah—besmirched his name with disparaging words, I wrote. The consequence was to have my tongue removed at the roots.

"Aaaaahhh!" They all screamed together, making my hand wobble.

Some girls have been known to live after such a surgery, but alas, I was not one of them. I bled without cease, no matter what poultice was applied to staunch the flow. Eventually I choked to death on my own blood.

"Eewww!"

That seemed a fitting ending. I tossed my head back and gurgled while my throat stretched toward the ceiling. The girls gasped, deliciously thrilled and horrified. Because we were seated on the bed, my forehead was spared collision when I threw myself forward. I merely sat hunched over, hiding my grin while their commotion buzzed above my head.

16

The palm symbolizes victory.

Girls nestled around me like puppies as I gazed up at the filmy canopy that hung over Lexie's bed. I'd never even changed into Mama's lovely nightdress. We'd slept in our clothes, exhausted by the drama of Gwendalen.

I slowly extricated myself without disturbing anyone and tiptoed downstairs, hoping to escape unseen. But Mrs. Johns was in the hallway, pulling on white gloves.

"An early bird, eh, Annie? Your little party sounded like quite a success last night, if giggles and squeals are any measure. Is that daughter of mine stirring?"

"No, ma'am. They're all asleep up there."

"Well, I'll have to go poke them." She laughed. "Sleep is no excuse to miss church."

"No, ma'am."

Church, I thought as I hurried away. I could do my good deed today. Mama liked to linger in bed on Sunday mornings—well, most mornings—so I did not meet her when I sneaked in to retrieve the bundle of clothes I'd collected.

The Wilky house sat at the end of a dusty road called the

Way. Each house along the Way got smaller and shabbier, with the Wilkys' being the shabbiest. No place I ever saw looked less likely as a waiting room for Heaven. No one out here had an automobile, so it didn't matter that the road was so badly rutted. I followed the straggle of people picking their way in Sunday shoes.

Along with my donation of clothing, I'd brought fifty cents to put in the basket, or the box, or the jar, whatever they had. They must have a collection, or what was the point? No spirits, God or otherwise, spoke loudly enough to drown out the clinking of coins. That was what Mama said, anyway.

Mrs. Tabitha Wilky answered the door. She wasn't wearing a badge declaring her name, but I could tell right off from her round eyes and disheveled hair that she was related to that girl.

"I haven't seen you before," she said.

"No," I said. "May I come in?"

She folded her arms across her chest like a sentry.

"What for?" she asked. She could use a lesson in appealing to potential customers, I thought.

"I was told the Lord makes an appearance here from time to time," I said. "Maybe I'll get lucky today."

She *humph*ed but leaned sideways to let me edge past.

The living room was just as Peg said, crowded with mismatched chairs and benches. The seats up front were full. Three or four people wearing white shawls were milling around at the front and humming. The choir, I guessed. I saw no sign of the minister or his daughter. I chose a stool near the door, in case I needed to flee. I tucked my bundle underneath.

I recognized two old women who drank lemonades outside Bing's every lunchtime and a man who sold newspapers near the train station. A few young women clustered together, sporting hats with jaunty artificial feathers, dyed lurid colors no bird ever wore. Looking around, I saw that the congregation was mostly women. Just like for Mama, I thought. Why are women the ones seeking answers?

I wasn't expecting much from the service, even less once the Reverend Wilky had shambled to the front of the room. His elbows were patched, and his trousers were flapping above naked ankles. What had happened to Peg's father's socks?

The choir quickly took their places in a semicircle around a rickety music stand. The Reverend Wilky stood waiting, looking like the scruffiest of mechanics.

But when he opened his mouth, oh, my! His voice was a low, rumbling burr, silky as he greeted us, his brethren. He began by rejoicing in the beauty of the day.

"And who made this day?" he asked.

Everyone around me called out, "He did!"

"Hallelujah! And who created this glorious sun?"

"He did!"

"Who gave us eyes to see the sky?" The Reverend's voice rose to a honeyed roar. The choir was humming a hymn behind him.

"He did!"

I joined in, having learned the routine.

"And who made our shoulders feel the sun after a day of labor?"

"He did!"

"Hallelujah!"

We were all with him now, warmed up, ready to go.

I'd heard that in most churches, the minister gave a sermon and the congregation sat as still as hymnbooks, listening to his mighty words, waiting to be transported to a holy place.

Here there were chairs, but once the service started, most people rose to their feet and stayed there, swaying, clapping, stomping, shouting and sweating, right along with the Reverend Wilky and possibly with the Lord above.

"Who sees that we are sinners?"

"He does!"

"Hallelujah! And who tells us how to punish the sins of our children?"

"He does!"

"Who tells us that to spare the rod is to spoil the child?"

"He does!"

"Hallelujah! He is here with us because we are all sinners! Because we are all spoiled and must face our punishment! Who is our only hope for salvation?"

"He is!"

"Hallelujah! And who here will accept His judgment? Who here will give whatever you have to follow our Lord to Heaven?"

"We will!"

"Hallelujah! Say it again!"

"We will!"

"Hallelujah!"

I knew the whole time it was a show. I was not persuaded

for a moment that God was listening in particular to Reverend Wilky of Peach Hill. But I was shouting and shaking and sweating. He was so good that I got to my feet and shimmied, nearly ready to stand up before the Lord along with the rest of them.

The ones who knew the routine shuffled their way to the front and dropped their money on a silver tray. They had the sweat wiped off their brows by the Reverend's own handkerchief in the middle of a blessing. Each worshipper took a sip or two of Wilky's Silk Revitalizing Elixir. More than one of them swooned right there on the floor and was dragged out of the aisle to be revitalized. I shuffled up with the rest of them and took a swig from the offered bottle. Wow! It scorched my throat and made my eyeballs hop. The man was serving straight-up alcohol, no doubt about it. The choir belted out music that grabbed the heart and tingled the soles of the feet; the tumult of salvation was overwhelming.

And then it was over. Reverend Wilky loped out the door. The chorus stopped and the singers gathered up their music sheets. Bodies flopped into chairs to recover, flapping prayer books like fans, noticing how hot the room had grown. Slowly, chatter took over from panting.

One of the choir members was staring at me. It took a whole minute to see that the pale, shining face with hair scraped back into a braid belonged to Helen Wilky, the wild girl. She'd surely undergone a Sunday transformation! I smiled in surprise, but she ignored me as soon as I recognized her, and she headed to the door.

The Reverend stood on the step outside with his family beside him, speaking with his flock as it dispersed.

"Greetings, sister." He sounded as if he had a sore throat. "The Lord is always pleased to see a new face."

"Greetings," mumbled his wife without looking up. She held a basket full of little bottles, each with a hand-printed label stuck on: WILKY'S SILK REVITALIZING ELIXIR.

"My name is Annie." I said it straight to the girl.

"Mmmm," she said.

"This is my daughter, Helen," said the Reverend. His fingers squeezed her shoulder and she winced. "A sinner, like the rest of us."

Helen bobbed her head and glowered at the ground.

A rush of recognition yanked me to attention. The Reverend Wilky's hand might as well have been holding the strings on a marionette. I'd been my mama's puppet too long not to notice, not to feel the tug myself. I knew there was a bruise under that choir shawl.

But the next worshipper was waiting.

"How do you do?" I said, and stepped into the mud of the front yard and along the Way.

Needle Street was simmering with activity. People milled about, calling to each other, chattering and giddy, as if they were at a picnic just waiting for the fellow with the hot dogs to appear. I ducked quickly back into a doorway. I had a feeling that I was the fellow with the hot dogs.

"Annie?"

"Peg!"

"I heard at church!" cried Peg. "You've had another episode! Lexie and her mother were full of the news."

"Oh," I said. "That explains the circus."

Peg's main concern was to check my focus, to make sure

124

the convulsions had not turned me back into a wonky-eyed moron.

"I'm all right, Peg. But . . ." I looked past her to the gathering people.

"We've got to get you safe inside," she said. "Where have you been?"

"Walking." Why mention the Wilkys' church?

"Your mama is going to wonder, she sees this crowd."

"My mama is going to fly off the handle, she sees this crowd. She doesn't like it when I get the attention."

"Maybe she'll think it's all for her?"

"We're not usually too popular on Sunday," I said. "Most people feel it's sneaking behind the Lord's back to seek solace from the dead on a Sunday."

Peg poked her head around the corner. "Oh, Lordy," she said. "We better go round by the alley."

Mama was just emerging from her bedroom as we crept through the kitchen door.

"Peg? Is something the matter? What are you doing here on your day off?"

Peg's eyes slid down the hall and back to me. "We met," she said. "On the corner."

Mama was too smart for that. She strode to the front door and opened it, ignoring Peg's cry of "No! Ma'am!" and slammed it shut when the crowd hallooed.

"What's happened?" She had me by the shoulders, her face three inches from mine. A muffled chant of "Annie! Annie!" rose outside.

"What have you done?"

"Gwendalen came back," I mumbled. "At Lexie's house."

125

"Lexie Johns goes to St. Alphonse Church," said Peg. "Her mother was telling the story up and down the pews, about the mutilated ghost that appeared on Lexie's bed."

Mama's temper caught fire like a match factory, and she shook me hard. Someone knocked at the door.

"Ma'am! No! You don't mean to be so fierce! The girl can't help herself if these fits come over her like that. Can she?"

What could Mama say? That she'd taught me to lie and I could help myself perfectly well?

"A talent like yours was bound to be passed on," Peg continued. "Your Annie seems to be gifted too. Isn't that a blessing?"

There came another knocking on the door, longer this time. Mama let go of me.

"Thank you for stopping by, Peg."

"Oh! You're right! My father will be wanting his Sunday luncheon. I'd better scoot." Peg left through the kitchen. Mama let loose.

"Do you plan to make a habit of treachery?"

"No, Mama! Please let me explain."

"I am the clairvoyant, Annie, no matter how you sneak about trying to steal the spotlight. When you healed yourself on a whim, I told you that I would not tolerate being undermined."

"I'm not undermining," I said. "I'm enhancing. There's a crowd of people out there, Mama. We can turn it straight into dollars. They think you healed me, so they expect me to be psychic as well."

"Well, you're not." She sounded as if she wanted to bite me.

Knock, knock, knock.

"But, Mama, don't you see? I could be. I could be anything we want me to be. We only have to decide what. There are two of us. We could double our offerings and double our income. . . ."

She turned her eyes to the door and seemed to be looking right through it.

"I suppose you think you're growing up," she said finally.

"It had to happen, Mama."

"Let them in," she said. "Palms only."

I opened the door.

"Palms only!" she called out. "We'll read you two at a time."

Mama took her lady into the front room, and I led a Mrs. Peers to the kitchen table. I held her hand in mine, noticing the polished nails, the gaudy bangles and the thin—meaning cheapskate husband—wedding band.

I took a moment, reminding myself: Heart Line, Head Line, Life Line, Mount of Saturn, and mounts of all the other planets.

"I see conflict under your roof," I said softly.

"That's my Bill," she sighed. "Scolding me day and night."

"Your heart line, here, shows an unhappy marriage," I said.

Her eyes filled up at once. "He never stops nagging! I spend too much money, I'm not cute anymore, I can't cook pork chops the way his mother does—"

"It's only your first marriage," I put in quickly. "There will be another, truer love."

"What? Really?" Mrs. Peers sniffed and wiped her eyes with the back of her other hand. "Who is it? Tell me!"

"His name is not written on your palm," I said. "But you will not travel to find him."

"He's a boy from town?"

"You may know him already," I said, "but you have not yet recognized his special place in your life." That would cover just about every possibility.

"What should I do?"

"While you're waiting to discover this love—"

"Yeah?"

"You are not a naughty child. Don't let your husband treat you like one. Remind your Bill that women now have the right to vote and you're running him out of office."

Miss Peers barked a surprised laugh. "You're a doll! "You're the cat's pajamas. I'm telling him tonight: Back off, buster! I've got a mystery man to find. Did you say he was dark-haired?"

"Sure," I said. "Dark."

"Here's your dollar," said Miss Peers. "Hold on, I'm gonna give you two. And I'm coming back next week!"

She clattered away down the hall, giggling as she tugged on her hat.

Could it be so wrong to give a person hope?

17

A spider repels plague when worn around the neck in a walnut shell.

On Monday, I was famous. Everyone had heard about me. Lexie, Jean and Ruthie waved at me as I came up School Street toward them, as if my footprints filled with rubies at every step. I even glanced back, imagining I'd missed an announcement and President Coolidge was arriving on my heels.

But really, I knew it was me they were waiting for. Gwendalen was the most amazing thing that had ever happened in Peach Hill. And for doing so little! Anyone who tried could convey messages from a lonely, tongueless medieval girl. They were simply too dull to bother. Mama always said that being dull was a far greater crime than being dishonest. I was escorted through the GIRLS door as though I were an exotic bird being carried to the king. No one spoke to me directly, of course. They chittered and buzzed as they always had.

In the hallway, I became the victim of numerous accidental collisions, as if my magic could rub off. Even teachers made excuses to speak to me. Lexie and her friends had taken care of telling the story, adding details and even chapters, until I hardly recognized my own creation: I had levitated off the bed and hovered near Lexie's ceiling, speaking a language much like Arabic; I had become a human magnet, compelling hairpins and spoons to fly across the room and attach themselves to my limbs; I had actually vanished in the dim light and returned with a severed head held in my waxy, outstretched hands. Oh, if only!

But there were scoffers, too. Delia de Groot cornered me after lessons, while Sally Carlaw stood guard a few feet away.

"Apparently you now claim that you were possessed by some kind of bleeding demon. Well, you should be locked up. You're as crazy as your mother. And you can tell her to keep her filthy Gypsy paws away from my father. He'd be better off arresting her than falling for whatever scheme she's hatching."

My hand itched to punch her pretty pink mouth. I pushed my fists deep into my jacket pockets and fiddled with the loose threads down there.

"I think you must be mistaken," I said, unnerved by how closely she skimmed the truth. "My mother is a professional."

Delia sneered. "And what exactly is her profession?"

I'd fallen into that one with my eyes wide open, letting her suggest that Mama was a whore.

"She helps people," I said, my voice sounding strangled even to my own ears. "Lonely people. Or lost. She could help find your mother, maybe."

"My mother is not lost," Delia hissed at me. "Not that it's

any of your beeswax. She's dead, as far as you're concerned, and don't I wish it were yours instead!"

I spun away from Delia, and Sally's smirking face next to hers. I ducked out the front door with my head down, not wanting anyone to see the tears splashing. I raced away from school, needing somewhere to hide.

I found sanctuary at the Peach Hill Public Library. The library had been a constant destination in other towns, but Mama had declared it off limits in Peach Hill because of my idiot disguise. She'd brought me books as part of my home learning, but I hadn't had a chance to roam the shelves myself. I stood between the stacks, breathing in the dusty paper smell, fingering the gilt-lettered spines of other worlds. It occurred to me that my new creation could be more authentic with just a little reading.

I looked up the accurate term for Gwendalen's punishment, dying to have it fall casually from my lips, if the pun can be excused. I devised that she had suffered an involuntary glossectomy (from the Greek *gloss*, meaning "tongue," and *tome*, meaning "to cut"). Looking through that book, I wished I hadn't killed her off quite so quickly; there were such lovely, grisly tortures that might have prolonged her ordeal and made for several dramatic sessions. I could have had the convent raided by barbarians or introduced the plague with its weeping sores.

At the desk, I ran smack into Mrs. Newman, waiting on line with Old Horse.

"Good afternoon, Annie!" she said. "I'd like to introduce my husband, Mr. Newman. Walter, this is young Annie Grackle, the girl I was telling you about."

"Ma'am," I said. "Sir."

Sammy was right; the man's teeth were enormous, the color of rancid butter.

I saw Mrs. Newman's eyes sliding over my stack of books: *Domestic Life in the Middle Ages, Herbalists and Bone Setters: Medieval Medics,* and *Saints Be Praised! A Guide to Medieval Religion.*

Her gaze shifted back to meet mine and rested there just long enough to make me squirm. "Nice to see you're getting interested in your studies."

"Yes, yes, I am," I said. "Did you know, for instance, that during the twelve hundreds, a girl my age was likely to be married with two dead children already?"

Old Horse grunted and then chuckled at my wit.

"Thank you for that tidbit, Annie," said Mrs. Newman. "I look forward to hearing how you make use of it in school."

As the Newmans left the library, old habit made my feet itch to follow them. Should I be a good girl and toddle home, or make use of this prize chance? It was too good to waste. I silently cursed the librarian for her ponderous attention as she checked out my books.

I didn't expect to welcome Mrs. Newman as a customer, but I'd started a file with her name at the top. Opportunity and plain curiosity now drove me to seek details. Outside, I could see the Newmans across the square, passing the church. I pinched myself for luck and headed after them, ducking behind trees and parked motorcars, keeping half a block back.

They were deep in conversation, making me bold enough to skip nearer and follow them onto Dash Road and into the grid of streets closer to the station and the factories. They marched along at a fair clip, chatting all the way. On Crossing Avenue they turned suddenly, going through a small gate and up the walk of number 157.

I stopped and reversed in a hurry. Heaven forbid they should notice me while fiddling with the key. I'd seen the bamboo shade in the upstairs window and a tabby cat sitting on the step. I'd seen Mrs. Newman smile at her husband as if his teeth didn't matter at all.

Sammy was waiting at the corner of Needle Street. He wore a new corduroy jacket, brown and soft looking, begging to be touched.

"Hey, Annie," he said. My heart jumped.

"Hello there. You weren't at school today." He'd missed my hour of glory.

"Toothache," he said. "But it's better now. Can you come for a walk?"

"Oh, I suppose," I said. I left the library books on the hall table and joined him back outside. Dusk was already darkening the sky, and I wished I had my gloves on.

"I hear you had a lively weekend," he said.

"Just the usual," I said. I am inhabited by seven-hundred-year-old glossectomized convent girls pretty much every Saturday night.

"Have you read any mystery stories by the great Sir Arthur Conan Doyle?" he asked.

"No," I said, wishing I could rave about "The Hound of the Baskervilles." "I didn't really learn to read until last week. I have some catching up to do."

"Oh, yeah." He paused while he probably remembered that until recently I was a chapped-lipped, wonky-eyed moron. "Well, he's a genius," he said. "He writes wonderful stories about a brilliant detective named Sherlock Holmes. The reason I'm telling you is that Sir Arthur Conan Doyle really believes in life after death, like the Egyptians believed. Only he's got scientific proof, not just faith."

"Proof?"

"He's got photographs of the ghost of his son, Kingsley, who died at the end of the Great War. Spirit photos, with Sir Arthur in front and the spirit dangling over his head in midair. Apparently lots of mediums take pictures during séances. They show phantom figures and mysterious lights and even ectoplasm oozing from noses or ears."

"That's disgusting," I said.

Mama and I knew about mediums who used ectoplasm—supposedly, spirits' bodily effusions—and swore it made their acts more convincing. I'd heard that Harry Houdini had found one woman pulling out yarn coated in egg yolk from a pouch in her corset. Mama said that was unsightly and refused to consider it. She said clients wanted to encounter the Other Side with elegance and dignity.

"But the evidence is captured on film," insisted Sammy. "That means it's real!"

Not necessarily, I thought. But perhaps Mama should learn something about photography and how to manipulate the results. Normally, she avoided having her picture taken, thinking too much publicity would lead to exposure. But she could make it alluring, part of the drama.

We had wandered back and forth across the square, under the statue of the mounted soldier.

"I'd love to see it," said Sammy. "You, going into a trance, I mean."

The chill on my back was not just the evening air. "It's my mother," I said. "Not me. She's the trance medium."

"Don't you think it's in the blood, that kind of thing? Like having straight teeth or stomach ailments? I'm sure you can do it too."

Of course I could do it, but blood was not involved. I'd been watching Mama all my life. It was theater, not science. I was leading Sammy on by not telling him the truth because I wanted him to look at me with his shining eyes, to think I was the most unusual and marvelous girl.

"I'm cold," I said. "And it must be suppertime."

"I'll walk you home," said Sammy.

"I'll be all right," I said. "I'll cut through the alley and be home in five minutes."

But he followed me out of the square and across Main Street. We entered the unlit pathway behind Lucky Ladies and the Blue Boy Bakery, where I'd first met Helen.

"Annie," he said. "Can you see in the dark?"

"I'm not a cat, Sam."

"I know, but I just wondered. Isn't it almost the same thing? Seeing into the future and seeing in the dark? We all know the path is there, but some of us are better at avoiding obstacles."

"I can't see into the future, either, Sammy. That's my mother, remember?"

"I have faith," said Sammy. Was faith worth having, I wondered, if it was based on deception? But his voice was low and warm and his arm brushed against mine, maybe on purpose. "I keep saying, I know you have the Gift."

"What if I don't?" I whispered. "What if it turns out that there's no such thing? Is that the only reason you like me?" It was dark enough for me to say it without blushing. I so wanted it not to be true. He stopped and leaned closer.

"Do you know what's going to happen in the next minute of your life?" he murmured.

Suddenly, Sammy and I were not who we'd been just a moment before. When he reached for me, we sank into each other. Hands and fingers, arms and shoulders melted together and we were kissing in the dark, kissing as if we'd done it a hundred times. It was best there was no light. I might have been too shy with light. But there we were, kissing, melting, kissing, with no one to see, especially us. We could just kiss. Until we stopped to breathe and the night got between our mouths enough to cool them.

"I'd better go." I was shivery and nervous, as if someone might turn a light on and spill our secret.

"Annie—"

I touched his hair in case there wasn't ever another chance, and turned to run with the feel of silk on my palm and panic in my throat.

I dared not look at Mama during supper, sure that she would see Sammy's imprint all over my face. But she had other things on her mind.

"Gregory is devoting himself to establishing connections.

136

I suspect it's an exciting change for him, not to be penned up in the dingy office of the stocking factory all day. . . ."

My ears wouldn't stick to Mama's words. I kept hearing Sammy: "Do you know what's going to happen in the next minute of your life?"

"He's a very smart man, you know," said Mama, fiddling with the pepper mill. "He has shares in a nickel mine in northern Ontario that expects outstanding results."

Was there any chance that Sammy could know it had been my first kiss? Had it been it his? Probably not, he was too good at it! I prayed that he'd never kissed Delia. I wanted to be first. And I wished I was kissing him again, right at that moment.

"I'm considering an investment," said Mama. "Since we've been so lucky in Peach Hill. We could double our money, Gregory says—"

I'd see Sammy the next day at school, but when would we have a chance to kiss again?

"Annie! You haven't touched your supper!"

18

If a strange dog begins to trail you, good luck will follow.

Getting dressed in the morning seemed more complicated when considered as the first step toward the next kiss. I dithered and cussed, not knowing what to wear and only having the same things to put on anyway. After the fourteenth or eighteenth time I'd fixed my hair, I felt a shiver of fear. Was I letting my brain go soft after only one kiss? I put on a white blouse and my gray wool skirt, lovingly stitched by Peg.

"I thought you understood," said Mama when I appeared in the hall. "We have work to do today. We're making preparations for our new performance schedule. Gregory is already arranging things. There will be no time for you to attend school."

"But Mama! I'll be in deep trouble for truancy!"

I have to see Sammy!

"I have to go to school!"

"Not today, nor any day in the future that I can foresee," she said. "And foreseeing the future is my business." She graced me with a tight smile. "You can remove that ridiculous garment. Eat your porridge and spend an hour going over your Latin verbs. Begin with 'to obey.' "

Pareo. I obey.

Parui. I have obeyed.

But not forever.

Fugio. I flee.

I needn't have wasted the morning cursing my mother; Mrs. Newman arrived just after lunch, when it was obvious that I was not merely late for school. I heard the knocker thudding and crept to the bedroom door to hear my fate.

"It is the law, Madame," I heard. "You have no choice. Unless your daughter has a letter from a physician, she must accompany me right now, or the police department will intervene."

I suspect that Mama made her decision entirely to avoid an interview with Officer de Groot.

"Annie!" she called. "Put that dreadful skirt back on!"

"Mrs. Newman, it wasn't my fault!" I trotted beside her, sneaking glances at the stern face, lips folded in and eyes glaring straight ahead. "I want to go to school! But my mother thinks that school is—is—"

"Yes, Miss *Grackle?*" Mrs. Newman stopped on the spot and scowled down at me. "What does your mother think?"

I bit my lip and looked away. "She thinks—she . . ."

What could I possibly say? My mother believes that school corrupts my loyalty and has forbidden me to waste time there. My mother has decided to sell my soul to a smarmy old man who will turn me into a performing monkey. My mother thinks that if I go to school, it will lead inevitably to her arrest and imprisonment. . . .

"I'm waiting, Miss Grackle." Mrs. Newman's fierce expression had not shifted.

"She is concerned for my health," I said. "She worries that the long days will tire me."

Mrs. Newman shook her head. "Utter nonsense. You are perfectly robust. I wish that you would tell me the facts of the matter, Annie. I am much better off with facts." She put a gloved hand under my chin. "Are you in a troubled situation? Do you need help?"

Oh, the beckoning truth!

But I spoke quickly, before I could cry or fling myself against her, pleading.

"No, ma'am. Everything's just fine. Shouldn't we hurry, as I've missed so much today already?"

Mrs. Newman sighed and began to walk without the vigor of anger in her stride.

"It is my duty to punish you for missing the morning lessons," she said in a flat voice. "You are assigned to detention and must report to the office after school today."

She did not speak again.

I took my seat in room 305, with only an hour left of the afternoon. I prayed that my hair did not stand on end from the electric crackle between Sammy's eyes and my heart. It was all I could do to keep my attention focused forward, especially as Delia's scalloped collar was the nearest scenery.

The teacher might have been speaking through a mouthful of buttons for all I understood. The glorious bell finally clanged to release us, though I pretended to hunt for a pencil in my desk, postponing the thrill of looking at Sammy.

"Miss Grackle?"

I jumped. I hadn't realized that Mr. Fanshawe was still in the room. Thank goodness I'd managed not to pounce on Sammy!

"Sir?"

"I understand you have a detention to address your poor punctuality?"

"Yes, sir."

"Then don't be late."

"No, sir."

Sammy followed me.

"When will I see you?" he whispered.

"Miss Grackle has an appointment." Mrs. Newman was waiting for me. My cheeks were surely scarlet.

"Yes, ma'am. G'bye, Annie."

Mrs. Newman led me down a narrow set of unpainted steps, through the boiler room and into an alcove, where she opened a gray metal door. The dungeon.

I paused, but her face remained stony, so I went in. The door was shut and locked in the same instant when I saw that the little room was not empty. Helen Wilky sat in a chair behind the desk with her feet up on the blotter. She was wearing my old shoes.

I glared at Helen with my arms crossed over my chest and

one heel kicking the door behind me. She was as stubborn as I was; we locked in eye-to-eye scowls while my heel went *thump, thump, thump.* Recalling my talent, I slowly crossed one eye. In reply, she grimaced like a chimpanzee. At last, we could only laugh.

"You ever been down here before?" she asked.

"No."

"Cozy, ain't it? Sorry I can't offer you a chair."

I slid down the wall until I was sitting. "I'm fine here, thanks," I said, though the stone floor was gritty and cold.

"She'll make us wait until we want to scream with boredom," said Helen. "Until we beg to go to class."

"But I want to go to class," I said. "I told her that. It's my mother who forbids it."

"I might have guessed," said Helen. "Newman sent a do-gooder in here to convert me."

"Why do you hate school so much?"

"Waste of time," said Helen.

"That's what my mother says. You'd rather be stealing buns from the Blue Boy?"

"Why not?"

" 'Thou shalt not steal,' " I said. "Aren't you a preacher's daughter?"

"That's why I do it," she said. "I steal as much as I can, whenever I can." She glanced around the empty room, as if she might find an atlas or a pencil worth pocketing. Then she looked back at me. "Who are you, anyway?"

"I moved to Peach Hill in August. My name is Annie."

"And your mother won't let you—oh, wait a minute—

your mother is the palm reader, ain't she? I saw you pulling loony that day." She started to laugh in funny short barks. "They're all hepped up about you calling in spirits. I heard about that and all I could think was, Nice scam! That beats my daddy hands down. And I'll bet you make money at it too, don'tcha?"

I was taken aback. I'd never met anyone so frank. I wasn't used to operating that way, saying what I actually thought.

"So your mother won't let you go to school. I'd have sworn my parents were the only crazies. Where's your father? Is he against school too?"

"He's dead," I said.

"Oh, the war?"

"Maybe," I said. "It's a bit of a mystery."

"My father is a raving lunatic," said Helen, as if she'd said "He likes jam with his toast." She added, "He brings the Lord into the living room in a frenzy of exultation twice each Sunday—well, you saw him—but he treats his family like worms under his boots."

"Why do you go along with it?" I asked. If she'd asked me the same question, how would I have answered?

"He's my daddy," she said. She picked at a scab on her elbow. "He frightens me. And what if he's right? What if Jesus Christ is watching our every move and our only chance to escape eternal damnation is to get saved every week? Like having a bath to scrub off the dirt?"

"That's a chilling idea." What if there really were an Other Side? What if the spirits were actually hovering nearby and ready to communicate? Not through my mother, of course, but through real sensitives, with true clairvoyant powers? Wouldn't they be watching Mama and me with gathering scorn and perhaps even a plan for vengeance?

"One of these days, though," mused Helen, "I'll be gone and you won't see me anymore."

"I left a bundle of clothing under my chair," I told her, blurting it out. "I thought you were the poor."

"That was you?" said Helen.

"You didn't have shoes. What did you do with Mrs. Newman's shoes?"

"I liked those," said Helen. "My mother snatched them. But I kept yours." She waggled her feet in the air above the desk. "Dunno what she needs shoes for, she hardly gets out of bed most days."

"Is she ill?"

"I'll say this much," said Helen, "she drinks her medicine every day. You've probably heard of the tonic my father makes? Wilky's Silk Revitalizing Elixir?"

"Oh, Wilky's Silky. Of course. Most popular drink in town."

"My mother is our best customer."

"But it's alcohol, isn't it?"

"Of course, what else would sell like that?"

"So—I don't mean to be rude, but if he sells so much tonic, then why . . . well . . . it's just that . . . what does he do with the money?"

"You mean why do we look like the poor?"

"I suppose that's what I mean. My mama thinks if you smell of success, people will be more inclined to trust you."

"My daddy's got all his money hid, stacks of it, someplace I haven't found yet."

"That's just like Mama!" I said. "Rolls of money, rolls and rolls. Only hers isn't hidden, it's tucked in every corner."

Helen stared. "Why don'tcha take it, then? Take it and go?"

"Never occurred to me," I said slowly, while I let it occur to me at last. "Would you really leave your family if you found the money? Where would you go?"

"I'd get on a train," said Helen. "I've watched trains lots, and thought about them flying through a hundred places in an afternoon. I'd wait till I saw a world where I wanted to live, and that's where I'd get off."

"And then what?"

"I'd find a room somewhere, where I'd be alone, nobody bothering me. Or maybe I'd have a dog. We had a dog, but he run off and got hisself killed."

"I used to know a dog," I said. "Trixie, in the carnival where we lived when I was little. Tricks by Trixie, right after the fire-eater. A dog is nice. But what about money? How would you live?"

"I'd just take stuff. I don't need much."

"But don't you want, well, to do something?"

"I . . . can't really do anything. Except, maybe, well, I can sing all right. Even my daddy says I sing like an angel. Maybe I could sing," she mumbled. "I just know what I don't want to do. No people and no God."

We heard the key grating in the lock. I stood up so that Mrs. Newman could open the door to come in. She stared without moving until Helen dragged her feet off the desk and stood up next to me.

"I hope your hour down here has reminded you both that time avoiding the classroom is wasted time indeed."

"Mmmm," said Helen.

"You don't have to convince me, Mrs. Newman," I said. Helen rolled her eyes and made a sucking noise.

Mrs. Newman did not bat an eye. "Every day that you're not in school," she said, "is another day that I track you down. Until you turn sixteen, the law insists that you attend school. For you, Miss Grackle, this is only a few days away. Miss Wilky, you have another year, and I will pursue you without rest. You are free to go. Good day."

She stepped aside. Helen darted out ahead of me and up the stairs like a lizard seeking sunshine.

"One more thing."

I looked back at Mrs. Newman.

"You'll have a difficult decision to make on your birthday, Annie. I urge you to speak with me if you need guidance. But I can't help you if you don't ask."

A train whistle echoed like an owl as I walked slowly toward Needle Street. Was this the world where I wanted to live? All these years of following Mama and never thinking about a life that might be different. Would it be braver to leave or to stay?

19

**Never speak ill of the dead,
but utter phrases such as
"poor man" or "rest her soul"—
otherwise the spirit may
come visiting.**

The streetlamps were illuminated by the time I went inside,
and the smell of gingerbread filled the air.

"I hope you whipped some cream, Peg!" I hollered.

But it was Mama who presided over the mixing bowl, wearing an apron and holding a bottle of vanilla in her right hand
as she whisked the cream with her left. Mama claimed the nuns
used to smack her left hand—they called it the Devil's Claw—
if she tried to use it for writing. But I wasn't so sure she didn't
train herself to favor the left, just to be contrary.

"Hello, dear heart," said Mama. Where was the morning's
exasperation? "Peg has not bothered to appear today, so I am
forced to make our supper."

"That doesn't seem like Peg. Maybe she's sick."

"You give her too much credit. It seems exactly like Peg.
She does the least amount of work she can get away with,
and now she has simply faded away."

"That's not fair, Mama."

"How was your afternoon in the halls of mediocrity?"

"Just fine." Why give her the satisfaction of hearing I'd had a detention? And why was I speaking to her at all? "Are we celebrating something?"

"Does it have to be a celebration for me to make my daughter's favorite cake?"

"Or a bribe," I said. "You imprisoned me this morning, so I don't trust you one bit."

Mama *tsk*ed at me. "So young and yet so jaded."

A knock on the door.

Bradley Barker's spotted face was entirely screened by an unwieldy cone of yellow lilies surrounded by baby's breath and ferns.

"More flowers?" I said.

"Could be the last ones," said Bradley, pushing the bouquet into my hands. "If the fella don't pay his bill, my uncle says."

"Thanks, Bradley." This time I found a quarter in my pocket and handed it over.

Why wasn't Mr. Poole paying his bill at the florist? My mind's eye skipped to the gold-link bracelet in the window at the jeweler. Was there a connection?

A little envelope was tucked between the leaves, and Mama showed me the card:

> Looking forward to an
> Enchanting Evening.
> With Gratitude,
>   Your devoted Gregory

She tapped the whisk on the edge of the bowl. "Here, you have the extra."

She handed the whisk to me like an ice cream cone. I took it warily, waiting for her to say what she was up to. Mama did not bake, even on birthdays, so this was going to be a lulu.

"I have some news," said Mama.

"Uh-huh," I said, licking.

"Mr. Poole has arranged our first performance."

"What?"

"Don't bleat, Annie. I do not respond to 'What?' "

"I beg your pardon, Mama, but aren't we moving a little quickly?"

"As you know, Mr. Poole is most eager to promote my talents. He has generously offered to begin with a soirée in his own home. Naturally, he knows all the prominent families in Peach Hill. It will be an important showcase for me."

"What happened to being discreet?" I asked. "Aren't we supposed to be steering clear of public danger instead of seeking it out?"

"We couldn't ask for a better debut."

"Debut, Mama? We've been doing this all my life. Why are you making it sound as though we need Mr. Poole? It seems to me that maybe he needs us for some reason. And what kind of act are you thinking of, exactly?"

"I will connect people with their lost ones on the Other Side. Let some spirits make guest appearances. We'll use the Envelope. It's so effective for a big crowd."

My heart sank. So much preparation, and so much left to chance.

"This is not a good idea, Mama."

"I have already agreed to perform on Saturday evening."

"Next Saturday? Four days away? I won't do it, Mama. I just won't. I don't want Mr. Poole to be our manager, and I'm shocked that you do. We've never let anyone do anything for us. You've been the one in charge. I won't work for him. You'll have to do the evening by yourself."

"Nonsense," she said. She tilted her head, softening, trying to win me over. "Mr. Poole has buckets of money, Annie. He knows about investments and savings bonds. Maybe I'm tired of being in charge. Maybe I want to be looked after too."

"Mama, I'm not so sure about those buckets. Seems pretty likely that they're not so full as he's letting you think."

"Why do you say that?"

"From odd remarks. I'm getting the picture of a man who may be in debt."

Mama laughed, relieved, it seemed. "Rich people are always in debt," she said. "That's how they get richer. They take risks. Gregory has explained all that. I may have been too careful to be clever with our finances."

"Are you planning something, Mama? Is this part of a bigger scheme? You're not still thinking of getting married, are you?"

She made a point of not answering, looking as innocent as the gingerbread she was scooping into bowls. Mama's idea of supper.

"I'm worried about Peg," I said.

"You'll have to get used to being without her," said Mama. "I've been considering a change, anyway."

"What do you mean? She only missed one afternoon, Mama. And she must have a good reason."

"This incident has only hastened the inevitable. We won't be needing her much longer." She smirked at me. "We'll be touring. We'll be leaving Peach Hill entirely. Unless we return someday to a house on the hill with a trained staff."

"No," I said.

"So I don't mind letting her go now."

"No," I said, stomping my boot.

"Oh, don't get huffy and storm about like a child," said Mama. "I've had enough of your histrionics. We can certainly come to an agreement, don't you think?"

I glared.

"I will permit Peg to remain in our employ, and you will perform with me at Mr. Poole's home on Saturday."

She had me. She'd tricked me and lied to me and she'd likely never even meant to fire Peg. But the trap had been laid and I'd fallen in.

"How much is he paying you?" I said.

She licked some whipped cream off her finger. "More than we've ever been paid for anything before."

Mama decided we would begin our rehearsals directly after supper. "We'll use the Envelope."

"But Mama, for the Envelope we need a Lurker."

A plant in the audience was what Mama called a Lurker. We used this trick only rarely, because a trustworthy Lurker was hard to find. Instead, we occasionally used people without their knowing it—Blind Lurkers.

"Maybe it's time to tell the truth to Mr. Poole," I said. "You could train him to be your partner, since you're so eager to have him look after things."

Mama lifted an eyebrow, considering my suggestion, it seemed to me. But then she patted my hand. "Don't be silly. A sweet-faced girl has much more audience appeal."

"I won't be sweet-faced much longer," I muttered. But I buckled down and practiced our code phrases and rehearsed the most common variations on spirit visitation.

As I did, I kept thinking, What is wrong with me? Why did I cooperate with Mama? Because . . . because . . . I'd always done it. Hadn't I been trained to be the perfect little partner? To do my bit to make the show better, to help Mama's star shine more brightly. Always in the wings, never expecting to take center stage.

I'd spent my life as a Blind Lurker.

By the end of our practice session, Mama was delighted with my precision.

"We'll set them on fire," she said. "Poor Peach Hill. They get the vaudeville players two weeks of the year, and a brass band on the Fourth of July. They'll be all agog for what we can offer. What else is there for entertainment? I can't imagine that Sunday morning with Monsignor O'Reilly at St. Alphonse counts as a rollicking good time."

I had to laugh.

Mama cocked her head. "I've always wanted to summon Jesus Christ from the Other Side," she said. "But it would have to be a very special occasion. . . ."

I didn't like to think about it, but Mama's high spirits

came from somewhere. Was it all because of the cash Mr. Poole promised, or did she actually like his grizzled cheeks and his coconutty hair? Did she get the same dizzy thrill from kissing him that I felt with Sammy?

Peg finally arrived late the next afternoon, with her eyes red-rimmed and puffy. She wore a shapeless black dress, and even her curls drooped.

"We're not on the telephone," she reported to Mama, "so I couldn't call to tell you. My father passed away yesterday, just after breakfast."

"Oh, Peg!" I flung my arms around her. Her shoulders heaved as she hugged me back.

"You're a dear one, Annie," she sniffed. "I know I've complained about him something terrible, the way he bossed me and worked me, but only a few hours gone and the silence over there is full of spooks, ringing in my ears."

"Oh, dear," said Mama. She'd been all set to give Peg a tongue-lashing, but now she had to swallow it and cough up gracious instead. "It's a very busy time for us, but I suppose you'd like a day or two off?"

"Oh, no, ma'am," said Peg, straightening up and wiping her face with her sleeve. "I wouldn't leave you without help. And I need the wages, ma'am. I need the money to bury him." The tears streamed down her cheeks.

I could see Mama didn't think we'd be getting much good labor anyway. "Annie needs exercise, Peg. She'll help you scrub the floors. Won't you, dear? As she's feeling so low?"

She floated back to the front room to continue her day of

feeding promises and consolation to strangers. Why couldn't she do that for the people nearest to her? I stuck out my tongue at her back.

We scrubbed the floor, all right, and the counters and the stovetop, and inside the darn oven.

"Peg," I said when we'd finally rinsed the buckets and put the kettle on. "Let's sit down. I want to read your palm. Your fortune is especially clear when you've just suffered a loss, did you know that?"

"Really?" said Peg. "I never heard that before."

"Well, it makes sense, doesn't it? Your emotions are churning, so your connection to the Other Side is heightened and of course your own path becomes more visible." Mama's gobbledegook.

Our hands were red and swollen from the morning's labors. I laid mine flat upon hers for a moment before I began.

"You have a long life ahead, Peg." I traced her Life Line, which was indeed a long one. "You've had much conflict under your roof, but it is now resolved."

"That's my dad gone," whispered Peg.

"Yes. But with him, I believe, went the obstacle on your Heart Line. . . ." I pointed to a tiny, meaningless crease. "After this, you see? The way is clear for romance, and you will find your true love."

"I will?"

"And it's possible you will not travel to find him."

"I won't?"

"You may know him already," I said, "but you have not yet recognized his special place in your life."

She giggled.

"You're a prize, Peg," I said. "You deserve some happiness."

"You do have the Gift, don't you, Annie?"

"Well, my mother taught me most things," I said.

Mama invited Peg to eat supper with us, knowing she wouldn't stay but making the gesture. We sent her home with a piece of ham. I tried not to think about her sitting at a lonely table staring at her father's slippers by the door.

It was after I'd done the washing up that I reached for the broom and disturbed the sugar sack that served as a bank. It was specially constructed, this bag of heavy muslin, to appear unopened, with a liner of real sugar to give the right feel, should Peg, or anyone, need to heft it out of the way. It usually held several hundred dollars. But the top was folded over, and when I picked it up, it weighed considerably less than it should.

"Mama?" I called, but then, "Never mind," when she answered me. A dreadful suspicion had seized me; all Mama's confident chatter about Mr. Poole's clever investments and doubling our money finally crackled in my ears with unnerving clarity. Had she given him a portion of our cash?

20

To dream of cake means you will have good fortune.

The supper on Saturday was a buffet, thank goodness. If I'd had to sit at a table next to one of those glittering matrons I would have choked. All that nonsense about salad forks and cheese knives that Mama thought I should know in case we ever entertained the President's wife, well, what did it really matter? A buffet was ideal, since I had no appetite anyway. I wished I wanted dessert; I watched one gentleman cram a chocolate cupcake into his mouth and look around for somewhere to hide the stem of the maraschino cherry. He flicked it onto the floor.

I perched in a corner, watching the dresses swish by.

Mr. Poole's niece, Miss Weather, wore a flapper dress the color of emeralds. I saw her flirting with Sally Carlaw's uncle Travis as if she'd invented eyelashes. Lexie's father was wearing a cummerbund the same silky crimson as his wife's corsage. Mr. Fletcher, principal of the high school, looked as though he'd last worn his tuxedo on his wedding day, a hundred years ago. Sally Carlaw had come with her uncle and brought along Delia, whose father was on duty at the police station. The de Groots likely weren't considered a better Peach Hill family, so Delia was lucky to be there. Her dress was gorgeous, I'll admit; a silvery gray shift, hemmed with a silky fringe. I wore black, as always, for the stage.

I never liked to perform in front of a scoffer, but it certainly wouldn't be the first time. The difference was that Delia was a scoffer I knew.

When supper ended, we were ushered into the ballroom, where a small jazz ensemble sat in one corner making sounds to set the mood, whatever mood that might be.

Mama called me to her side. I had barely been able to look at her that week, since my notion of distrust had taken hold. Though she didn't know the reason, she had not been pleased with my manner. We'd been testy with each other on every occasion.

Her eyes now were wide and fond, her public devotion at odds with the quiet threat in her words.

"You will make this work, Annie. We are a team. Do not forget that."

No one watching would notice anything amiss. Mama licked her fingertips and smoothed my hair. She pinched my cheeks to make them rosy. "Be a good girl," she said. "Be a doll."

Mr. Poole had set up a little platform, decorated with a fringed carpet and a potted palm taller than Mama.

She perched on a stool with the toes of her beaded slippers dangling. She wanted to stay alert and upright. She was flushed and pretty, eager to start. It took an age for everyone to find a place, and then Mr. Poole tapped a spoon against a wineglass and cleared his throat.

"It has been my great pleasure these past few weeks," he said, "to make the acquaintance of our newest Peach Hill resident." The smattering of applause muffled a remark from the back that I suspect was lewd.

"And my delight has only increased," Mr. Poole went on, a little more loudly, "as I have come to admire her extraordinary gift."

There was a flutter of curiosity. The invitation had not been precise, saying only that guests would never forget what they were to see here tonight.

"We live in remarkable times!" Mr. Poole was booming now, all warmed up. "The human mind has invented and explained so many things. Who would have imagined, when I was a boy, that man would fly in airplanes, let alone fight a great war from the sky? Who would have thought that a message could be telegraphed or a conversation spoken through wires across the Atlantic Ocean? The very fact that it is night and we sit in a room illuminated by electric lights is reason enough to believe in miracles. So why do we suspect that the brain might falter in the face of mere death?

"This has been a matter under serious study by many leading scientists. Even Thomas Edison spent his later years developing a machine to receive spirit messages. If only he had been so fortunate as we are, to know a trance medium who would undergo observation upon request . . ."

Mr. Poole gestured toward Mama, full of pride. "You will be astonished, as I have been, at the ease and accuracy with which Madame Caterina displays her talent. I urge each of you to seek her guidance on any matter that requires discretion.

"This evening, we will witness a demonstration of her remarkable ability to read minds and to contact those of our loved ones who have left us and now dwell on the Other Side."

His introduction had caused a breathless hush of anticipation. Mama was beaming. Even I felt quite pink, as if we really were about to contact spirits from beyond. I would never have guessed that beating under Mr. Poole's well-cut coat was the heart of a carnival barker.

The basket that held our supplies sat beside the doorway. I scooped it up and made my way amongst the chairs, distributing paper, envelopes and small pencils as Mr. Poole continued.

"To assist with the demonstration, we request that you write down a question, or the name of a person you have lost, and then seal your paper into an envelope. Madame Caterina's lovely assistant"—he smiled at me—"her daughter, Annie, will come around and collect the sealed envelopes."

Mama and I had discussed it a hundred times—should we engage a Lurker or not? I'd finally convinced her that it wasn't worth the risk, but now the pressure was all on me. It was up to my sharp eyes to find the one word we needed to begin.

I shuffled between the rows and collected envelopes. The audience was beginning to chatter again, intrigued and suspicious and merry with the fun of Mr. Poole's inventive game. Mama's gaze met mine across the room of scribbling guests. My stomach began to tighten. The prickles I felt before any performance raced up and down my arms as I circled close to the "stage."

"Have you got me a name?" said Mama between smiling teeth.

I scurried into the audience to fetch the last few envelopes. I caught sight of the letter "E" just as a woman folded her paper, with probably a "d" and then some other letters. As I handed the brimming basket back to Mama, I whispered, "Ed."

Mama handed her silky flame-colored scarf to Mr. Poole to tie around her eyes.

"I am honored indeed," he announced, "to introduce to you Madame Caterina!"

The applause burst out like firecrackers all over the room. Mr. Poole stepped off the platform and left us to it.

My mother sat blindfolded and perfectly still until the racket settled down. She was as cool as a lake breeze. I couldn't bear it if something went wrong, but in the same minute, I prayed for that to happen. Why should things always go her way?

Seconds ticked by while the audience held its breath. Mama reached out her hand, and I passed her the first envelope. She displayed it in front of her, stroking it dramatically, humming softly at the same time.

"I am receiving a strong message from a person whose name begins with an 'E,'" said Mama. "Please signal if this means something to you." Thankfully, the woman whose note I'd spied on lifted her arm. I went to her side and was engulfed in the scent of lily of the valley.

"The person is recognized, madame." That was code for "It's a woman." If it had been a man, I would have said, "The person has been identified."

"Ask her to stand for a moment," said Mama, "to clear the air around her. I believe her caller will make an appearance." Some people didn't realize straightaway that Mama had divined the person as a woman, but the whisper went through the room pretty quickly, rustling like yellow leaves.

"The reception is not entirely clear," said Mama. "Is it Edward?"

"Edmund!" called the lady with a shake in her voice. She already had a lace-bordered hankie at her lips; she was ready to crumble.

"He seems to be upset about something. Do you know what this might be?"

"Oh!" the lady cried. "He didn't have a chance to tell me good-bye! He was taken sudden."

"Yes, yes," said Mama. "It was unexpected." She so naturally repeated whatever the person told her that it sounded like psychic wisdom.

"He went one afternoon to buy a new trowel for his gardening. He had a seizure and passed on, right there at Murray's Hardware, next to the nail bins."

"Edmund has been waiting nearby," said Mama. "He's here tonight to say farewell. Do you have a message for him?"

The woman groped to support herself on the chair in front of her. "Edmund!" she hollered. "Ed! It's me, Mildred."

"He's waving," said Mama, "with a look of great fondness."

161

"Good-bye, Ed. Forgive me—I nagged about your personal habits, but you were a kind man. Good-bye, dear." She slumped back into her seat and blew her nose loudly. She dabbed her eyes and nodded at the onlookers. Whether they were amazed or skeptical, it didn't matter. Mildred's grief was clearly eased. And it was only the first act.

Mama pushed her blindfold up to her forehead and handed the envelope to me. I tore it neatly across one end, withdrew the paper and handed it back to her, but not before I'd glimpsed the written word "Michael."

"Edmund!" My mother pretended to read, silently enlisting "Michael" as the next ghost.

"Oh!" the audience murmured.

Mama chose another envelope from the offered basket and slipped her blindfold back in place. She went through the trembling, stroking, humming routine again.

"Michael has come to visit," said Mama after a respectful pause of several seconds. "Would anyone here be awaiting Michael?"

"That's my boy," said a man gruffly.

"That's my father," said a woman, jumping up.

"He seems to be quite a young man," said Mama, always preferring the story more likely to twist their heartstrings.

"That's my boy," said the man again. "He was nineteen. Died in the war."

"But he's laughing," said Mama. "Why is that?"

"Oh, he was a sunny boy, our Mike," said the man. He reached down to pat the arm of someone sitting next to him, and I realized it must be Mike's mother, with tears trickling down her face.

"Perhaps the medium can give you both some comfort," I said, letting Mama know there were two of them.

"I feel that his good humor was a morale booster for his fellow soldiers," said Mama. "And he wants you to know he did not suffer at the end."

"But they told us he was left wounded on the battlefield," said the man. "For two days with his leg shot off."

Oh, cats! We couldn't pay for a sadder story! The hush in the room was like the gulp before a sob.

My neck burned. We were despicable cheats, using people's deepest sorrow for entertainment.

But . . . so good at it!

"He did not suffer," Mama said, hurrying on, "because he knew your love was with him throughout the ordeal. His last earthly thoughts were of your home."

Mike's mother shook with sobs. Her husband sat down and put a bulky arm around her narrow shoulders. A good start, with two crying women.

Again the torn-open envelope, again the paper passed from me to Mama. It was a question this time, but I did not have a chance to read it.

"*Michael!*" announced Mama, and then replaced her blindfold. What next?

She held the envelope as before, but this time her hand shook, as if she trembled with emotion.

"The person who asked this question urgently wants an answer!" Mama smiled. "The spirit world is responding with a simple reply, loudly and clearly. *Yes,* you will find a husband! And without too much more waiting!"

Not one but two ladies jumped to their feet, each

exclaiming that it was her question. Mama laughed along with the rest of us. "No wonder the spirits were so adamant," she said. "There must be two husbands waiting. In fact"—she pulled the scarf away from her eyes and let her hand hover, quivering over the basket—"am I sensing a husband in this very room?" Her eyelashes fluttered prettily, as if she were the wife-in-waiting.

A young man wearing spectacles and a violent blush raised his hand from the second row. "That's me," he said. "My question. I was only wondering." He shrugged.

"Well, now you have your choice of two!" said Mama. I could see how pleased she was that she'd hit the bull's-eye. "That is perhaps the quickest delivery on a promise I have ever managed!"

Oh, they loved her now. She tore open the envelope and read aloud: " 'Will I ever find a husband?' " The audience clapped. Mama slid on the blindfold and I placed another envelope in her hands.

"I am receiving another name," she said. "Please show yourself, without speaking, if you are related to someone passed over named Carol. Or, perhaps, Caroline?"

A man heaved himself to his feet.

"The person has been identified, Madame," I said. I thought I recognized him as one of the gents who worked at the bank.

"Sir," said Mama. "You have lost someone?"

"Caroline," he said. "My sister."

"Yes, of course," said Mama. "She has something to tell you. She seems to be shaking her head. Do you understand her message?"

"Can't say as I do," said Caroline's brother. "You tell me. You're the genie."

A scoffer. Some people seemed to think that if they challenged a medium, it made them look clever. Mr. Poole stood up near the wall, as if preparing to pounce if he didn't like the fellow's attitude.

"I am a clairvoyant," said my mother gently. "Not a genie. Genies are magical creatures who live for hundreds of years. I hope you are not implying, sir, that I appear to be a century old?" Everyone laughed, charmed. Someone in the back even gave one of those wolfish, admiring whistles.

"But Caroline is still trying to reach you," added Mama, calming the audience. "I feel that she wants to prevent you from doing something you are contemplating. What might that be?"

"As if I'd tell you," said the man, flushing.

"Absolutely right," said Mama. "You deserve your privacy. I'll tell your sister to keep her advice to herself."

"You do that," the man blurted. "What's she giving advice for, anyway? She died when she was two!"

Another laugh from the audience, embarrassed this time. The man was pouring vinegar on Mama's show.

Mama pushed up the blindfold and ripped the seal on the envelope. She scanned the paper quickly as she passed it to me, urging me to pretend to read it. The words on the page read, "Will the person I've lost come home?" What I read aloud was *Caroline!*

The applause was not so noisy or prolonged this time. We needed a good ending. Mama replaced the scarf over her eyes.

"I am hearing a question that speaks of heartbreak," she

165

said. "You have lost someone and have trouble accepting that there will be no return."

A hand shot up in the back. I made my way toward it. My heart thudded to the polished parquet floor.

"The person is recognized, Madame."

It was Delia de Groot.

21

She who hurries cannot walk with dignity.

"My mother is gone." Delia stood to make her declaration.

Her mother wasn't dead! Half the people in the room knew that! But Mama had no idea who had spoken, and she was already responding.

"I see her beckoning to you, as if she has a secret to tell," said Mama.

A wave of snickering rippled through the hall. She had a secret, all right. Delia blanched. Mama hesitated, confused.

I cut in. "Madame is contacting only the deceased this evening," I said loudly. "She is skilled at finding missing persons, or objects, but she is currently envisioning the Other Side and not prepared to seek out what you have lost."

Delia narrowed her eyes, almost beaten, but then leaned forward, as if ready to pounce.

"Then how did she see my mother 'beckoning' in the first place? She's a phony, that's how! You're fakes and liars, both of you, phonies and fakes!"

The people all around her shifted in their chairs, gaping

in excited horror, as if watching a wrestling match. Mr. Poole hurried over but then stood useless and dithering.

I admit there was a part of me that gaped in admiration. Delia was doing what I'd never have the nerve to do: taking on Mama, and in public! But only for an instant. We were in peril, and I knew what should be done with Delia. Toss her through the French doors! I wanted to bellow. Dunk her in the pond!

Mama tore off her blindfold, her cheeks glowing and her eyes locking on their quarry. Go on, Mama! Chew her up and spit her out!

Mama pulled herself up tall, set her shoulders back and took a slow breath, while everyone else was holding theirs.

"You're very young, miss," Mama began quietly. "Your experience of the phenomenal is limited—"

Delia stomped her foot. "Show me the papers! Show us the notes you were reading. I'm sure there's a trick!"

The paper Delia had written was in my pocket. The others were on the floor around the base of the stool. Her paper should still be in its envelope. What if she kicked up enough of a fuss to have us searched?

But Mama lifted a warning finger, like a schoolmistress. As long as she had a smidgeon of control, there would be no scoffers scrambling for evidence.

"What lies out of our sight is often beyond our understanding." Mama raised her voice a little, putting music into it, so that it carried above the chatter. "We expect the spirit world to be mysterious. Understanding the nature of loss is a lifelong challenge. But when a loved one leaves us, *by choice*, instead of through death, it is most difficult to accept."

Delia flinched, but Mama continued, calmly exacting her revenge.

"The missing person hovers in an emotional mist, becoming a memory before her time, instead of remaining a presence. She is standing offstage, as it were, overlapping with those we cherish on the Other Side."

"You're lying!" shouted Delia, fists clenched and face aflame. "This is babble!"

"Memories are the spirits we create for ourselves," Mama said firmly. "The recollection of your mother is trapped by your desire to see her again." She was almost purring, though her heart must be thumping, as mine was, like the heart of a hurdler galloping to the last jump. She stepped to the edge of the platform. "I can locate her roaming aura, if you care to consult me privately." The audience chuckled. "It may be that her situation is one you do not care to share with all of Peach Hill. . . ."

Delia sat, deflated.

Mr. Poole appeared at Mama's side. "My friends, Madame Caterina!"

Mildred, widow of Edmund, rose to her feet, clapping. A few others joined her in a sprinkling of applause, though not the hurrahs and cheers that I knew Mama had hoped for.

"Champagne is being served in the next room." There came a well-timed *pop!* "Please join me in a toast to the marvelous Madame Caterina!"

Mama curtsied gracefully and left the stage. She would never cry, of course, but her eyes burned with disappointment. I pretended not to see her beckoning me. Instead, I followed Delia into the hallway, where she waited with Sally to receive her wrap from Norah. Demanding an apology was meaningless, I knew. I wanted to yank her hair or rip the tassels off her shimmering dress.

"Delia!"

But when she looked at me, I saw the face of a sad little girl, spite and haughtiness flown away.

"Delia?"

"Are you happy now?" said Sally. "With your mother making a fool of her in front of everyone?"

"But she—you—" I decided to ignore Sally. "You were bent on destruction. You purposely tried to make fools of us first. Mama just turned the tables, and not very far."

People streamed out of the ballroom, pressing around us, far too many for Norah to assist by herself. Sally's uncle Travis waved from the door to tell her that their car was waiting.

"I don't like liars," said Delia. "Especially mother liars." She hugged her shawl close around her shoulders.

Me neither, I thought. How did she know?

A little of Delia's old spirit had returned. "And your mother is the biggest liar of all," she said. "Except possibly for Mr. Slippery-Slidey Poole. She deserves whatever she gets. I'm going now." She took Sally's arm as they squeezed through the crowd toward the door.

What?

The foyer was full of flashing jewels and happy chatter. Mr. Poole, everybody said so, was a charming host and threw a splendid party. Madame Caterina had been a treat, so pretty and surprising.

I felt as if my skin were crawling with spiders. What did

170

Delia know about Mr. Poole? Or was she guessing, like me? She had often been horribly right about things. Had my mother given him money? Were our hard-earned bundles of bills hidden somewhere inside this house? The curving staircase beckoned. One small person slipping out of the crowd would hardly be noticed, would she? I was halfway up the carpeted steps, compelled to prowl.

"Annie?"

"Oh!" I about jumped out of my shoes. It was Mr. Poole, standing suddenly on the landing above me.

"The upstairs is strictly off limits to guests, my dear. Even special guests."

"I—I—was looking for the ladies' room."

"Indeed. It remains, as during your last visit, behind the second door on your right in the lower corridor."

I stepped down one step.

"Your mother asked me to give you a message."

"My mother? Has she gone?"

"Well, yes. She was disheartened by events. I had Douglas drive her home. She said you would understand."

"She left me here?"

"I'll have Douglas take you when you're ready."

"We suffer a disaster and she abandons me?"

"Nonsense, child. It was hardly a disaster. Your mother is the most extraordinary woman I've ever met." He clasped his hands across his heart to emphasize how thrilling she was.

"Not according to everyone," I muttered.

"Ah, yes. That brings me to the next point." He came down the stairs, glancing past me at the hallway brimming with guests. He put his hand on my arm, guiding me toward a door that opened into what must be his study. "May I have a word with you in confidence?"

If I'd believed in ghosts, I'd have said that one had sauntered through me right then, the chill I got.

The room was dim, with enormous armchairs flanking a cold fireplace. The floor was littered with boxes and stacks of books, as if the library were being moved.

"Events this evening have led me to question what I believed about you and Catherine," said Mr. Poole. "That snip suggested that your mother is not a genuine medium. That she employs tricks to captivate her customers." He gazed at me intently, making me feel as if I were shrinking to the size of a mushroom.

"Delia is disturbed," I said. "About her own mother. It makes her feel better to belittle mine."

"I'm not certain that is the whole of it," said Mr. Poole.

"The natural ability of a psychic must occasionally be enhanced by theatrics to have the desired impact," I said carefully. "Is that what you're referring to?"

Mr. Poole smiled. "You do take after your mother, don't you? She can spin gold out of words." He kept pausing between sentences, making me shiver.

"Your mother was splendid when I met her," he said. "I'd never visited a psychic before. I . . . I imagined she could expel my wife's nagging ghost, perhaps make some business predictions. I trusted her."

Why was he telling me this? How could my mother have left me here?

"But now it appears that trust was misplaced."

I shuffled my feet, inching back toward the door. Would they hear me in the foyer if I began to scream?

"Now!" He flung his arms up and tossed back his silvery chin. "Now the sun is rising in the west! We are looking at the world from a different hilltop! Far from being less than what she was, she is much more!

"She enchants whomever she encounters. She is not ruled by the whims of unreliable spirits who may or may not materialize; she decides who will visit and when! Such cleverness! Such charm!"

He put a confiding arm around my shoulder. "Her only error is one we can quickly address. Her only error is that she performs her magic for mere dollars when there are hundreds and thousands of dollars available for such a talent as hers."

"It's not an error," I said. "It's the way we work. We are best—Mama is best—with one person at a time."

"Not anymore," said Mr. Poole.

"Mama doesn't want to be famous, or to attract dangerous attention."

"I don't think you understand," he said, his voice like honey. "I have plans for Madame Caterina. What you've done in the past, what you think you want or don't want; none of that matters. I am now equipped with knowledge that could lead to your undoing. Best to avoid that, don't you think? Together we can flourish. As long as you follow instructions, we will all be very rich! We'll leave Peach Hill far behind. Is this clear?"

My hands were like ice.

"Douglas must be back by now; I'll have him take you home. Be sure to tell your mother about our little chat."

I wanted to think before I passed on any messages. Messages? Threats. He'd threatened me. Both of us. This was exactly why we'd never trusted anyone. There was a reason we had that rule, and I didn't intend to waver now. But for the first time, I didn't trust Mama, either. She seemed to go right along with him. I couldn't read her the way I used to; I wasn't seeing everything. Had she given him some of our money to invest in a dubious nickel mine? Did she really want to go with him on a tour that might spark unwanted attention? Would she marry him?

I found Mama sitting at the kitchen table, staring at the wall as if it were a train window with the whole world hurtling by. I slid into the other chair, deciding to be sulky about being left behind.

"Don't be petulant." Mama cut me off before I could complain. "It was essential that I leave before strangling that hussy. What I don't understand," she said, "is why she took such personal delight in humiliating me."

"Mama, she doesn't want you to seduce her father. She doesn't want you for her mama. Isn't it obvious?"

Mama looked aghast. "Surely not! What a revolting idea!"

"It's funny," I said, "because she seems to be right so much of the time. It's just that her intent is evil."

I stopped. Was it evil? Or simply . . . self-preserving? Like the rest of us?

* * *

Sunday passed with no customers. We were tired, and it was a relief to have a quiet Sunday. The knocker clacked once, to announce Douglas, burdened with a case of leftover champagne and one of the floral arrangements from the buffet table. Mama was quite cheered up by the note.

> Forever amazed,
> Always devoted,
> On to the next . . .
>
> Gregory

22

If you sing before seven, you will cry before eleven.

I woke up on Monday, my sixteenth birthday, to hear Mama singing. It was unusual enough that she was awake before me, but singing!

"Happy birthday, darling." She patted my cheek and put a bowl of freshly sliced pears on the table. "Many happy returns of the day."

"Thank you, Mama." I ate a piece of fruit.

"Do you think I look any older?" she asked.

"You? No, Mama, you never do. You're just as beautiful as you were yesterday."

"I think in our next town you should stop calling me Mama. I think we could be sisters, don't you? You might practice using 'Catherine' around the house."

The pear jammed in my throat. "Our next town?"

"We'll be going on tour very soon," said Mama. "We were thinking we'd head south for the winter. Go to sunny places where it smells like orange blossoms whenever you open the window. Gregory has already contacted certain acquaintances. He's coming over after breakfast to devise the itinerary. We can all sit down to look at the map."

I couldn't let this go on. I had to stop her. I had to stop him.

"Mama, I have to tell you something about Mr. Poole."

She went still.

I took a breath. He knows about us, I wanted to say. We have to run away again. But that was exactly what I didn't want. I wanted, with all my heart, to stay in Peach Hill.

"I don't trust him," I said, whispering. "He's acting as if we're indebted to him, as if we belong to him somehow."

"Annie, you trust me, don't you? My instincts are telling me that this tour is exactly what we need. We'll keep moving, always ahead of scrutiny. Gregory is certain the rewards will be tremendous. Have I ever led us wrong?"

"But Mama—"

"Try using 'Catherine.'"

I couldn't depend on her listening to me. Somehow I'd have to prove that he was not to be counted on, find some evidence that shouted "steer clear" . . .

I volleyed one more excuse, guaranteed she'd find it a poor one. "We've hardly been here yet. What about my friends?"

"Every town has friends," she said, flipping her hand. "And now that you're sixteen, we can stop worrying about school."

"I'm going to school, Mama. You can examine the map without me."

"Legally, you are no longer required to attend school." She leveled a look at me. But it was my sixteenth birthday, and I could be ruthless too.

"I'm going to school because I want to be there. I like it. I'm learning everything that you never taught me. The world is wider than just us. I need to know it all. Oh, and look at the time! Thanks for the lovely breakfast."

Sixteen! I bounded into Needle Street. I was going to school! I would devise a scheme to unmask Mr. Poole. We would not succumb to blackmail. I would not spend the rest of my life scurrying from town to town like a vagabond. Whatever happened later, however she worked her black magic, at least I'd told my mother that I was going to school!

Sammy was waiting on the corner.

"Is it true?" he wanted to know at once.

"Is what true? What did you hear, Sammy?"

"At the bash on the hill. Your mother saw ghosts while she was wearing a blindfold, but then Delia got up and called her a sham."

"What do you believe? My story or Delia's?"

"I haven't heard yours yet."

"I'm getting a little tired of explaining myself," I said, sounding way too much like Mama. "You'll have to decide for yourself."

For Sammy to like me, he had to believe that I was a psychic. For me to like Sammy, I had to pretend that he was smart enough to know I wasn't a psychic. It was getting confusing. I still just wanted to kiss him every time I saw him.

Not only Sammy had heard the scandal, of course. As with all other small-town dramas, reports of Mr. Poole's party crackled through Peach Hill. Delia's version was the main source of gossip for the high school.

"You were faking?" Lexie and Jean accosted me on School Street as Sammy sidled away. "It was all a hoax? Delia told us everything!"

"Delia doesn't know everything," I said. "Why would you believe Delia? She's been saying her mother is dead for two years when really everyone knows that she ran away with— oh, never mind!" I could play just as dirty as Delia.

Lexie and Jean gaped.

"With who?" said Jean.

"You mean it's true?" asked Lexie. "About the fellow who sells fish? I heard my mother and her card friends talking. You mean it's true?"

"Delia is not to be trusted," I said in a dramatic whisper. "She has a turbulent episode coming on, according to the cards. Emotionally very unstable."

"How do we know that's not just another lie?"

"You know what you saw, don't you?"

"Do we?" said Lexie.

"She couldn't possibly have faked that, Lexie!" said Jean. "She went terribly ugly. Nobody would do that if it weren't real."

Shouts and laughter brought us up short at the school gate. Helen Wilky, standing on one foot, was circled by jeering schoolmates. Frankie Romero held one of Helen's shoes—used-to-be-my shoes—high above his nasty, grinning head. I confess to one moment's relief that it wasn't me inside that crowd of sneering faces, but that didn't stop my mouth.

"What are you doing?" I hollered. "You put down that shoe, Frankie Romero, or you'll be in deep trouble!"

"Ooooh! It's the Gypsy princess," announced Delia. "Making a prediction!"

I squinted at the row of gaping faces: Sally, Howie, Pitts and Delia, joined by Lexie, Jean, Sammy and several others. I strode right up to Frankie and slammed my fists against his shoulders.

"Let go of that shoe, you bully!"

He lowered his arms but kept dangling the shoe from his finger.

"You better do as she says, Frankie," said Delia. "She'll put a hex on you."

Helen snatched her shoe from Frankie and darted away from his grabbing hand. She would have kept running, but the big door swung open and Miss Primley's arm began to ring the bell. I pulled Helen over to sit next to me on the bottom step while the others filed inside.

"Another reason to avoid school," said Helen, tying her shoelace. "But thanks." The toes of her shoes were scuffed and muddy, looking much worse than when I'd had them.

"Helen, I wonder if you would help me with something." She narrowed her eyes, suspicious.

"It's—it's—I need you because there may be"—I was whispering—"stealing involved."

Helen barked that odd laugh of hers. "I can do that. Where and when?"

"The Poole house," I whispered. "Tonight, I hope. Eight o'clock? If I can be sure that he's going out."

"What, the old geezer who's courting your mother?" She didn't bother to keep her voice down. "The ruckus that

Delia's been blabbing about? This gets better and better. What are we looking for?"

"Don't say 'courting,' " I said. "And I won't know till I see it, what I'm hoping to find."

"Excuse me?"

We spun around. Delia de Groot was standing on the top step. "Miss Primley said to get inside or be marked late and she'll call Mrs. Newman."

I worried through mathematics whether Delia had eavesdropped before she'd spoken. I worried through geography about how I would arrange for Mr. Poole to be far from his mansion on Hill Road that evening. I worried through chemistry that I should never have told so much to Helen Wilky, notorious sneak thief. I worried through English that perhaps I'd lost my mind. My mother wouldn't give money to Mr. Poole for a risky investment, would she? She was far too smart to be fleeced. Wasn't she?

"Mama?" I said, coming in after school.

Peg poked her face out of the kitchen and pointed to the front room. "She's in there, with that Mrs. Peers of yours. You come on in here and get yourself a birthday blessing." Peg hugged me hard and laid down a bowl of warm apple crumble.

"Your mama's been cranky," she said, "until that Mr. Poole called on the telephone. There hasn't been a customer all day till this one. Mrs. Peers asked for you, but your mama told her no waiting. You better keep right out of sight."

Peg lit a candle and stuck it in the crumble so I could make a birthday wish.

"Don't tell me!" she said. "You want it to come true, don't you?"

Let me have the life I choose. I blew out the candle.

We heard Mrs. Peers leave, and Mama came in, shaking her head at me. "I don't know what claptrap you fed that woman, Annie, but she is intent on seducing the dark-haired postman."

"It's right there on her palm, Mama." I tilted my head to remind her that Peg was listening. "At least, I saw she had a romance looming. She decided who to tackle."

"Peg, I will have my bath and prepare for this evening. If by some miracle we have another caller, fix a time for to-morrow."

"Yes'm." Peg took my empty bowl and wiped a cloth across the tabletop.

"What are you doing, Mama?"

"I know it's your birthday, dear heart, but I didn't think you'd mind. I'm going out to dine, with Gregory."

"Really?" The prelude to my wish come true!

He'd be safely out of his house, but he'd also be telling Mama he was on to us. Would he threaten her, too? Would she come hurrying home to drag out the carpetbags, ready for flight? All I needed was something to wave in his face to force his retreat instead of ours.

If I could find papers, or a statement from the bank, showing that his finances were not as healthy as he pre-tended . . . Even if I could find a stash of twenty-dollar bills and reclaim them as our own . . .

"I hope he takes you somewhere fancy," I said, to cover the pause. "And maybe dancing. I know you like that."

"You're being very generous," said Mama. "I know your feelings for Gregory are not the warmest."

Peg raised her eyebrows at me over Mama's head and left to draw the bath.

23

Laugh alone and the world thinks you're an idiot.

I met Helen at the school gate and we walked up the hill together. Mr. Poole's house looked bigger now that I was approaching it as a fortress to be breached.

"Looks high, doesn't it?" I knew by now that the wrought iron fence did not restrain a lurking dog, but it was still a six-foot fence.

"We climb over," said Helen, not the least bit daunted. "We smash one of the panes on those fancy garden doors. We knock out the jagged bit with a stone and poke a hand through to jiggle open the handle."

I stared at her. "You sound a little too sure that would work," I said. "But breaking glass would be too noisy. The maid would hear us." That gave me an idea. "I think you still get to climb the fence, though. Good thing you wore your dungarees." I'd worn my trousers too, but I didn't plan to crawl over the fence.

"And where will you be?"

"I'm going to see if I can get in through the kitchen. I

know the maid, a little, hopefully well enough. You wait at the French doors in the garden, and I'll meet you there. But stay hidden and don't smash anything!"

Helen hoisted herself over the fence, and I trotted around the corner to the servants' entrance. The light was on in the cellar kitchen, and Norah came out to the gate a moment after I'd rung the bell.

"Oh," she said, "it's you, is it, miss?"

"Hello, Norah," I said. "My mother thinks she may have dropped an earring last night. Did you find it, by any chance? A pearl drop set in gold?"

"No, miss."

"May I go and take a quick look?"

"The master's not here."

Well, I know that!

"And Douglas, he's driving. Since the chauffeur was let go."

"I'll only be a minute," I said. "I just want to check around the platform where she was performing."

"I suppose . . ."

"Thank you, Norah! You don't have to lose your suds," I said, pointing at the sink, where she'd been washing the dishes. "I'll go up and be back before you've finished rinsing the last cup."

"I suppose . . ." She nodded toward the stairs, and I took them at a ladylike gallop.

I found myself in the foyer, with the only light coming from a glimmering chandelier above my head. We'd used the dining room for the séance the first evening. I hurried across its dim length to unlatch the first pair of French doors.

Helen appeared at once and slipped inside with a grin.

185

"Stay here," I whispered. "Open the door for me in five minutes."

I raced back down to the kitchen, where Norah was just drying her hands.

"No luck," I said, shrugging. "Thank you anyway."

"Yes, miss."

"Good-night, Norah."

Instead of going out by the gate, I scuttled around the side of the house, through the pagoda and straight to the French doors. *Tap, tap.*

I was in! We stood in the dark, shaking with excitement and in a fit of giggles, if Helen's wheezing qualified as giggles.

"Let's go." I led her into the foyer and hesitated.

I wanted to search Mr. Poole's study, where papers and files would most likely be. But was it wise to send Helen upstairs by herself?

"You're looking for cash," I said. "Twenty-dollar bills. You can't go through taking just anything, okay? We have to be discreet."

"Mmmm," said Helen.

"I mean it," I said. "We're trying to prove that he's a cad, not get ourselves arrested."

Helen tiptoed up the staircase. I hopped across the carpet to the room where Mr. Poole had taken me on Saturday night.

The door was locked. Oh, rats! Locked! Of course. Why hadn't I thought of that? And the key was probably jingling about in his pocket right now while he ate caviar with my mother. I turned and hurried up the stairs after Helen.

My first surprise was on the landing; the beautiful Persian

runner that carpeted the treads stopped abruptly as the stairs turned for the second flight. My shoes now clicked on bare wood. The floor of the upstairs corridor was bare. There were no paintings on the walls and no shades over the lights, no ornamental tables, no chairs, no mirrors.

"Helen?" I called in a whisper.

The nearest door opened into an empty room. Moonlight shone through uncurtained windows, making my shadow the only decoration on the wall. The next room had been a library or reading room. There were shelves from floor to ceiling, but they held only a few battered books with unstitched spines or stained covers, the remnants of a collection. Room after room looked nearly abandoned.

"Helen?"

"Here." Helen beckoned from a doorway ahead of me. Mr. Poole's bedroom had a majestic bed covered with a royal blue eiderdown and a dozen plump pillows.

Helen pointed at a row of boxes on the chest of drawers in the dressing alcove, the sort of boxes that would normally hold jewelry. She lifted the lids and tipped them over. Not one coin, cuff link or ring tumbled out.

"He's sold it all," said Helen, "I bet you! He's got no more money from what his wife left him. He's been selling off or pawning whatever he had."

"All his wife's jewelry," I said, remembering the bracelet in the shop window. "All the books and the paintings, even the furniture and rugs. No surprise he thinks she's haunting him—he's got a guilty conscience. Maybe his investments are duds. The study's locked. There's no way to look at papers or find Mama's money."

"He's only pretending he's rich," said Helen. "There's nothing to take! What a waste!" She kicked the shoe rack, which held a dozen pairs of shoes in different shades of brown. It toppled over with a resounding *thunk, thunk, thunk* as each of the shoes hit the floor.

Helen's face showed the alarm I felt. "Oh! I didn't mean to do that!" she cried out. Our clattering race back down the corridor was not nearly so careful as our arrival.

"Stop!" I hissed at the top of the stairs. "Wait! Norah is all the way at the bottom of the house. Maybe she didn't hear anything."

We stood still as stones for more than a minute, listening for footsteps, or bells, or screams. Nothing. The house nearly trembled with quiet.

"Let's get out of here," I said. "It's making my spine prickle." I led the way down, relieved when my shoes hit carpet again and I could breathe. Until, *creak* . . .

My heart stopped. I felt Helen freeze behind me. Norah's frightened eyes peered out from the door that led to the kitchen.

"You, miss? I thought you'd gone. We said good-night, didn't we? Didn't you leave already? You've scared ten years off my old age!"

I tried to smile, tried to summon ease, tried to think what to say as I descended to the foyer.

And then the worst words of all. "I've telephoned to the police," said Norah. "And let Mr. Poole know at the restaurant that he's to come straight home."

Half a glance behind me showed that Helen had vanished. She must be hiding on the landing, waiting to hear what would come next.

"You better come to the kitchen with me, miss, and explain to the master, else I'll be in hot water up to my eyeballs."

"No," I said. "I . . . I'll go outside . . . I'll tell them it was all a mistake. You go on to the kitchen and I'll speak with the police as soon as they get here."

I strode to the front door, hoping I looked confident, blameless. Norah retreated down the kitchen stairs.

Helen's head popped up over the railing, and she tore down the stairs in seconds.

"Don't use the front walk," I whispered. "They'll be here any moment." We trotted across the lawn, away from the front gate.

Helen swung herself over the fence in a blink, landing softly on the other side.

"Come on," she said.

"I should stay," I said. "Norah knows it was me."

"Don't be an idiot," said Helen. "Let them find you later, safe home in bed." I laughed out loud. I tried to heave myself up, but my feet kept slipping on the palings. Helen put her hands through the fence to give me a boost, and I swung one leg over the top just as a whistle pierced the night. Out of the shadows half a block away up Hill Road came two uniformed men, waving their sticks and hollering.

"We're cooked," said Helen.

"Run!" I said. "I mean it, run!"

She ran down the hill faster than a rabbit in front of a

greyhound. I yanked my other leg over the fence, tearing the silk of my trousers as I thudded to the ground.

A motorcar trundled up the road, beeping its horn, at the same moment that Officer Rankin laid his nightstick firmly across the back of my neck as a warning not to move.

Happy birthday, I thought.

24

It is a good omen to meet an idiot when on some important task.

Officer de Groot apparently made a brief attempt to pursue Helen, but he was back, puffing heavily, within a minute. The same minute it took for Douglas to open the doors of the automobile and assist Mr. Poole and my mother to climb down and come barreling over to investigate.

"What the devil's going on here?" demanded Mr. Poole.

"Catherine?" Officer de Groot was still puffing, but I could hear the dismay in his voice.

"We discovered two youths trespassing on your property, Mr. Poole, sir," said Officer Rankin.

"Catherine, what are you doing here?"

"Hello, Monty." Mama paused. The be-kind-to-men-in-uniform rule was about to backfire.

"She's with me," interrupted Mr. Poole. "If it's any of your business."

"So you were not at home this evening, sir?" Officer Rankin was trying to conduct his inquiry.

"We were dining out," growled Mr. Poole.

I could hear a small cluster of neighbors gathering.

"Douglas," said Mr. Poole, "go check on your wife. Make sure all is secure inside."

"Yes, sir." Footsteps thudded away.

"We received a telephone call at eight-fourteen p.m.," said Officer Rankin. "From a Mrs. Douglas."

"That's right," said Mr. Poole. "I got the same call. Noises, burglars, thumps."

"And looky here what we found. Ruffians climbing out over the fence. One of them got away, being faster than—"

"Did you get a look at the one who managed to escape?" asked Mr. Poole.

"No," admitted Delia's father.

"Up you get, boy." Officer Rankin tapped his stick against my back, and Officer de Groot dragged me upright by the arm.

"Annie!" cried Mama.

"What the—"

"Annie?" said Mr. Poole. "What the hell are you doing here?" I didn't know which way to look. Mr. Poole's face was twisted up and much too close. Mama showed astonishment, but she was quickly determining her next step, I could see. The police officers—well, confusion overtook them.

"What are you doing on my property?" thundered Mr. Poole. "Did you break into my house?"

"Gregory!"

I needed more time to think. I started to whimper and then sob. A sympathetic "*Ahhh*" rose from the audience across the road.

Mama opened her arms and folded me inside. "Have you

192

hurt my child? Did you lay a hand on her?" The spectators murmured as she assumed the role of outraged mother.

"No, ma'am," said Officer Rankin. "But she is a suspect in our custody, and I'll have to ask you to release—"

"Nonsense," said Mama, holding me closer than she had in years. I shut my eyes. What should I be doing? "There is clearly some misunderstanding, and—"

"Let go of the girl!" Officer de Groot bellowed suddenly, surprising us all. Mama loosened her embrace but kept me next to her, with her arm linked through mine.

"No need to be so fierce, Monty!"

"I am an officer of the law," he growled. "You will address me accordingly. We've had a report of a break-in. We found this child climbing a fence in the dark, along with whoever it was that got away. We have a little digging to do here. We're going down to the station to ask questions until we get to the bottom of this!"

Douglas appeared at that moment, jogging to his master's side.

"Well, Douglas?" asked Mr. Poole. "Is Norah all right?"

"She's in a state, sir. Hard to get a clear story. And there's a bit of an upset with your shoes, sir, nothing else."

Now they were all staring. Even the neighbors had inched themselves to the middle of the quiet road, intent on watching the scene unfold.

Mr. Poole's voice was low and hard, as threatening as the rattle of a snake's tail.

"What were you doing in my house? What were you looking for? What did you see?"

I felt Mama tremble. She gazed at me, her face only

inches away in the gloom. She crossed her eyes, ever so quickly, and made her lips go slack. The policemen both stepped nearer. My mother blinked as the faintest smile flitted across her mouth. She knew we needed a pause, a chance to synchronize our efforts.

She reached for the blue-clad arm of Officer de Groot and drew him close to her, ready to spill a secret.

"This is very difficult for me, Monty." Her voice was husky with quickly produced emotion. "This experience has done greater damage than you've realized. Look at my daughter! The fall, the dreadful nightstick, who knows what? But she has had a serious relapse! Her mind has left her!"

Mama turned to me, dipping her chin ever so slightly, a signal that I should take center stage. I didn't think. I did what I'd been doing all my life, especially in a crisis; I obeyed Mama. I clapped the heels of my hands together. I panted, then squawked like a pigeon in great distress. I gurgled and stomped my foot a dozen times as if I were trying to wipe my boot.

The onlookers gasped. Mr. Poole struck a hand to his forehead. Officer Rankin coughed. Mama winked at me, she was so proud.

"Uh . . ."

The fearless police officers looked at each other.

"Uh . . ."

Mr. Poole narrowed his eyes and stepped in close, examining every droop and pucker of my face. His very stubble was bristling with anger.

"You—" he began.

But Mama put a restraining hand on his arm as she pleaded with the police.

"She needs to go home," she said. "She's terribly hurt."

"She doesn't look well," admitted Officer Rankin.

"She broke into my house, Catherine!" Mr. Poole's frustration was giving me the giggles. "What was she doing in there?"

I was betting that even if he'd confessed to Mama earlier in the evening that he knew of her admirable deceit, he certainly wouldn't have admitted that he was broke, would he? That was why he was in such a tizzy, I was sure of it.

"Look at her, Gregory! What harm could she possibly have done? Perhaps she felt this dreadful fit coming on and came searching for her mother! She needs to go home."

Another of Mama's rules: Retreat from outsiders to put our stories in line. I allowed a glob of spittle to roll over my lip and down my chin.

"Uh . . . ," said Officer de Groot. "Maybe, uh, the interview can wait until tomorrow." His partner shuddered and nodded.

"Thank you, Officers." Mama pressed a palm to her bosom. "An act of human kindness."

Mr. Poole grasped her arm and pulled her to one side, pulling me too, as I was attached to Mama.

"What's going on here, Catherine? Is this part of the game? I'd like to know what she was up to in there."

"I'm surprised at you, Gregory. You must realize that my daughter is every bit as trustworthy as I am."

"Is she indeed?" said Mr. Poole. "Drive them home, Douglas."

25

It is bad luck to leave a house through a different door than the one used to enter.

"We were having a lovely evening before the telephone call from his maid," Mama started as soon as we were indoors. "He said he had something very important to discuss with me, and—"

"Mama, stop," I said. "I know what he was going to tell you, and it's connected to what I did tonight." I felt it all bubbling up, ready to gush out in a torrent, but I forced myself to slow down. She wouldn't listen if I rattled her. I had to lead her through it carefully, as if we were climbing rickety stairs.

"Well?"

"He knows about us," I said. "About you."

"What about me?"

"Mama!" Why was she making me say it? "That we're not really in contact with the Other Side," I said. "That you're a fake, like Delia said."

I watched her absorb that much.

"How does he know?"

"He just figured it out," I said. "But that's not the important part." Mama's pride was wounded, I could tell. She so depended on being the best. "The important thing is that he still thinks you're brilliant. He is more enchanted than ever."

When did my mother learn to simper? She must actually like this man!

"I'm pretty sure that's what he was going to tell you at dinner tonight."

Mama's thoughts were dancing across her face, until she hit the ugly question. "And how does this relate to your becoming a common burglar?"

"I had to investigate, Mama. Too many things weren't adding up. And I was right. He has no money. That's what he's trying to hide. His fancy house is half empty. He's behind in his bills and he's selling his possessions. You are a fresh source of income. . . ."

She snapped her head up and held me with icy eyes.

"I'm sorry, Mama. I'm sure he likes you, too. I know he does. But he wants to be our manager so he can take our fortune."

I whispered the next part. "You gave him money already, didn't you, Mama? From the sugar sack?"

She would never answer that question out loud, but I knew. She squeezed her eyes shut for an instant, and her shoulders gave an involuntary shudder before she straightened up again.

"Well, that's that," she said, crisp and certain.

"Not quite," I said. She cocked her head inquiringly.

"He knows about us," I repeated. "He's with us or he's against us, you see what I mean?"

"Ah," said Mama. "Aha!" And she started to laugh. Suddenly, she clapped her hands together as if I'd given her a prize.

"Gregory Sebastian Poole," she said, "you've met your match."

The knocking came scarcely later than dawn, rousing us both. We huddled in the hallway.

"It could be Gregory," whispered Mama, "come to confess."

I crept into the front room and peeked out the window, catching a flash of copper buttons.

"It's the police!" I hissed, just as another knock was heard.

"Oh, pish," said Mama. "We can manage the police." She opened the door, and in stepped Officer de Groot, with his partner close behind. I shrank back into the parlor, eager to listen but not wanting to be seen in my nightdress.

"Uh, oh, Madame, oh, Cath—uh, I hope we're not, well, of course we are, disturbing you?"

And they called me the idiot? Between Mama's satin wrapper and tumbled hair, he didn't know where to put his eyes.

"Good morning, Officers. This is a little earlier than I had expected you."

"Tell you the truth," said Officer Rankin, "it was the gentleman, Mr. Poole, who suggested we come by early, in case you had a trip in mind."

Mama's eyes found mine peeking out from behind the door. She hid her grin with a haughty glare. "Indeed? Well, here we are, as you can see."

"Yes, ma'am," said Officer Rankin. "But what he also said, ma'am, was that if you answered the door at all, that is to say, if you hadn't made a run for it, then we were to consider you both innocent of all suspicion. It was a childish prank, he said."

Mama signaled and I reluctantly appeared, with my eye askew and my mouth pretending it belonged to a fish.

"And my daughter so frightened that she has become an imbecile again?" said Mama. "How do I cope with that?"

"We're very sorry, ma'am. We don't understand how that happened. We did nothing to harm the girl." Officer Rankin seemed genuinely remorseful.

"The whole episode is puzzling to me," he went on. "But I've learned one thing in all my years on the force: the darkest secrets have the smallest doorways. And that just makes me search all the harder for the key."

That was not a comforting thought. But Mama managed a graceful farewell and sent them on their way.

"And now the day lies before us," she said, stretching. "I think I may go back to bed for a while, until Gregory calls. You can do the same, darling, since you can't go to school. . . ."

Oh, no!

"But Mama, we're safe now. Can't I just say I woke up and I was better?"

"No, Annie, and don't you get fussy on me. The stars are now aligned to put this latest tragic episode to some good use. You will remain in this condition until I decide otherwise."

What had I done? I had slammed a door and locked it. I couldn't gallop off to school. I was an idiot. I really was a fool.

We might have escaped from one difficult situation, but I was Mama's prisoner again.

When Peg arrived, she found me hiding in my room. "Oh, my poor little Annie." She scooped me up and murmured into my hair. I felt sick. She'd already heard the news. Everyone in Peach Hill heard everything. "I hate to think what must have happened to shut your brain down."

She could maybe help me, if I told her the truth right then.

"Peg," I said.

"Peg loves you, honey. You understand that, don't you? As addled as you are?" She whispered slowly and clearly, the way she'd always done before, when I was an imbecile.

I nodded. I couldn't tell her. It wasn't only today; it was all the other days, and weeks, when I'd been a wonky-eyed, chapped-lipped moron. I'd lied to Peg a hundred times. Why would she bother to let me explain?

"Don't pamper the child," said Mama from the doorway. "This misfortune has befallen her because of disobedient and deceitful behavior."

"But ma'am—"

"She is to be left alone."

Peg stroked my hair.

Mama tapped her toe until Peg was in the hall.

"I can help you, ma'am," said Peg. "We'll set things up the same and make it work all over again."

"What are you talking about?"

"You'll be wanting to mend her like you did the last time. Heal her, with a miracle."

"Well, no, Peg, not at once. I'm not ready—she's not—"

"She's not herself, is what she's not. But you got the Gift, ma'am. You just say those prayers again, and put your hands on her shoulders, and she'll be right as rain."

"As I said, Peg, she brought this on herself. She can live with the consequences for a few days, as far as I'm concerned."

Peg's silence was like electricity. I sat on the edge of my bed, realizing the cold truth. Even if I really had been an idiot, even if Mama had been able to heal me, she would have chosen not to because there was nobody there to watch.

"You may let in the first customer, Peg," said Mama. "And make appointments with the rest, every half hour as usual."

"But there's no one out there, ma'am." Peg's voice seemed to come from a stranger.

"What do you mean, no one?"

"I mean not a living human being stands outside that door, ma'am."

Ooh, Peg, I thought. Mama doesn't like being sassed.

I heard my mother's swift steps and the sound of the door opening and closing. Peg was muttering in the kitchen, "You think I lost my marbles too? You think I went blind overnight? You think I don't know what 'no one' means?"

I almost laughed out loud. I could hear her cussing and banging the cupboard doors. She still could not believe what she'd just heard falling out of my mother's mouth.

Mama was back in the kitchen. "There's no one out there."

"As I was saying," said Peg.

"I don't understand. How could there be nobody?"

"You asking because you want an answer or just asking?" said Peg.

Mama's voice was sharp. "Do you have something to say, Peg?"

Oh, Peg! Please don't! She needed this job.

"No, ma'am."

Peg went about her chores while Mama paced and checked the street yet again in case a troupe of fortune-seeking housewives should appear, waving their palms before them. Peg brought me lunch on a tray. We heard Mama pick up the telephone receiver to listen for a moment before clunking it down.

"The telephone works fine," said Peg, "just like it did five minutes ago, last time she checked."

I looked at her.

"Just nobody calling, that's all."

"I'll thank you to keep your opinion to yourself, Peg," snapped Mama, coming into the bedroom.

Peg looked sideways at me. "Not an opinion," she said. "It's a fact. It's Annie they want to tell their fortunes. But she's been unhealed and back to stupid, so why would they come to you, if you can't help your own daughter?"

"That will be all, Peg. You are excused." Mama spoke as if she were spitting ice. "Permanently."

Peg stood up like a duchess and left the room.

"No!" I cried, scrambling to follow her. Peg took off her apron and plucked her coat from its hook.

"Peg loves Annie," she said, gathering her handbag.

"Annie loves Peg," I said.

She crossed the kitchen floor and stepped out the back

door, with her chin tipped up to the storm clouds. I watched with an ache in my heart so fierce I thought I might choke.

"Well, now," said Mama. "That's done."

"She'll talk, Mama," I said, fighting the wobble in my voice. "This won't make things better."

"I won't have servants sassing me."

"She only—"

" 'Only' is too much," said Mama.

There was a knock. We looked at each other. Mama went to answer, praying for a client. Rain pattered against the kitchen window.

"Oh, it's you," I heard her say. "My daughter is ill. And beyond that, she is now sixteen and no longer attending school."

I crept forward along the hall.

"I'm interested in her welfare, despite her age," Mrs. Newman said. "This is merely a friendly inquiry. Oh! Annie! Hello. Your classmates have been asking about you, worried that you're not in school." Sammy?

"With good reason, as you see," said Mama. Her hand around my shoulder managed to pinch. "Annie has suffered a dreadful fit. She has always been a sensitive child."

I tried a loony grin, but my eyes filled up, and I bit my lip to keep the tears from spilling.

Mrs. Newman looked at me closely. "I'm sorry to hear that you're not well," she said. "Your friend Helen was also absent today."

"Well, thank you very much, then, Mrs. Newman," said Mama briskly. "Good of you to visit. Annie needs her rest now."

I touched Mrs. Newman's arm as Mama opened the door. Both of them stared at me. I was certain Mrs. Newman knew I had something to say, but so did Mama. They were watching every move I made. As the truant officer stepped into the drizzle on Needle Street, I tugged at her sleeve.

"Mrs. Newman!" My dimwit voice was too loud, like a honking goose. Mama moved in, ready to pounce. Mrs. Newman was flustered with both of us so close.

"Please telephone if you need anything," she said to Mama, but I knew she meant it for me. "Oxford two three six two."

There is an instant after a match has been struck before the flame ignites. Waiting for Mrs. Newman to trot out of earshot, I felt that about-to-be-burning moment. Mama yanked me inside and shut the door with a smack.

"You were trying to tell her something."

"No, Mama."

"You are doing everything you can think of to destroy me," she said quietly.

"No, Mama. That's not true."

"When did you stop listening to me? When did you begin to have your own opinions about everything?"

There came another thump at the door. Mama sighed. Her hopes for a customer were dimming. I crept backward to my bedroom, not wanting to playact anymore.

"Ma'am?" I kept my door open to listen. "Is this where Annie lives?" Sammy!

"And if it is?" Mama had abandoned her charm.

"I'd like to speak with her, please."

"That won't be possible," said Mama. "She's ill."

"But could I just see her?" Dear Sammy. "I—uh—I brought her an assignment from school. Some reading."

"No," said Mama. "She's ill. She won't be returning to school."

"What? But then I have to see her. She's my—I'm her—I mean, we're—"

No, Sammy! Don't say it! My palms went clammy as I clutched the door frame.

"Are you telling me that you're a special friend of Annie's?"

"Uh, yes, I guess so."

"Annie?"

Oh, no!

"Annie? Come out here, please!"

I shut the door of my room with a bang and threw myself onto the bed. How could she? She couldn't!

The door flew open and Mama scorched me with a whispered tirade. "You come into the hall this instant and you give that handsome boy a look at his sweetheart; a creeping sneak, a disobedient liar and a cross-eyed fool!"

Her fingernails dug into my shoulder as she dragged me upright by my blouse.

"You get out there and be repulsive or I will cross your eyes permanently!"

Sammy flinched when he saw me coming. With my left eye wobbling, nose red from crying, mouth agape and heart splintering into a hundred pieces, I was not the sweetheart he'd kissed behind the Blue Boy Bakery.

"Hoi!" I leered through tear-puffed eyes and waved, as sweetly odd as I could manage. Sammy just stared. Mama patted my shoulder, still tingling from her grip.

"You see, son? Annie has had a little setback and will not be at school again. Thank you for stopping by." Mama opened the door.

"But—but—ma'am! Can't you fix her, like you did before? Please, ma'am?" He was so urgent, my tears came trickling out again.

"I've been praying, son. Naturally, there is nothing I wish for more."

"Sammy!" I whispered. Mama's fingers closed in a pinch. I could almost feel my skin turning purple.

"I'm sure it means a great deal to her that you came over. Good-bye."

He retreated into the street. He tossed me one more anguished look and hurried away, black hair flying.

I slammed the door and bawled, huge gulping bellows. Mama slapped me, *thwack*, across the cheek. "You're hysterical."

I gulped.

"I hate you!" I'd never said anything I meant so passionately.

"The only good to come of this," said Mama, "is that now we can have a public healing, where everyone is watching!"

"No!" I said. "I will not do that! You can't make me!"

Mama just laughed. "You'll see."

I went straight back to my bed, praying that I could sob myself into oblivion. Could she have done anything more cruel? Sammy's eyes haunted me. They'd been full of disgust.

But I didn't sleep, of course. The hours ticked by while the same questions rang inside my head. Had Mama always been cruel and I hadn't noticed? Why did I see it now? What could I do to save myself?

Helen knew all about the trials of heartless parents. I would find Helen. Maybe she could tell me what to do.

26

If you cut bread unevenly, you have been telling lies.

No reason to disturb my mother. I bundled on an extra sweater under my jacket and began the long hike out to the Way. Clouds raced across the moon, blown by a fierce wind. Light dipped or shone in brief turns.

I was no more than halfway there when I saw her, small and hunched and limping toward me. Her gait was uneven and slow.

"Helen?" The wind sucked the word and took it the wrong way, so I was almost on top of her before she heard me calling again. "Helen!"

One look at her face told a terrible story. Even with the shifting shadows, I saw that her right cheek was red and misshapen, her eye a dark crack in a swollen blue egg.

"Oh, no."

She was wearing a man's plaid shirt over her dungarees, wrapped across her skimpy body, held closed with a belt. A felt pouch was tied to the belt with string.

"What happened? Who did this to you?"

"He never touched my face before," said Helen, struggling to make her lips move properly. "It wouldn't look right on Sunday."

"He? You mean your father? He hits you? Where was your mother? Why didn't she stop him?"

"She was drunk," whispered Helen. "She can't do anything when she's drunk."

"Wilky's Silky," I said.

"The best thing she did last night was to pass out on the floor so'd he trip and fall on top of her." Helen paused to run the tip of her tongue slowly over her lips. "That gave me a minute, so's I could go to my room. I rammed a chair under the doorknob and prayed to that Lord of his to smite him into cinders."

"Holy Hell."

"That's it exactly." Helen croaked out a laugh and then winced. "Holy Hell." She shivered and pulled the shirt tighter around her. "I've been skimming the collection, so I've got some money, just not all of it."

"Is that what ticked him off?"

She looked at me, suddenly accusing. "No! It was you! I forgot! It's your fault. You musta told that creepy rat policeman that I was with you."

"No, it wasn't me! I swear, I never would! I think it was Delia. She heard us at school, out on the steps, remember?"

"He came looking for me, poking around, making my father crazy. Daddy's a small operation, they don't bother him usually, they never busted up the still or anything." Helen licked her lips again and kept going. "But this time the copper kept asking me questions with the Rev standing there, so he knew I'd done something coulda made lots of trouble."

"I was coming to find you," I said. "Does it hurt too much to move?"

"He got in one whack at the backs of my knees," said Helen. "Before I kicked and ran. It's achy but not so bad. I'm okay to walk, I think."

"You can lean on me if you need to. Let's just go, so we're not so close to your house."

"Where we going?"

"Your face is a mess. You should go to a doctor."

"You know I can't do that."

Who could look after her? Mama was out of the question. Peg was the one. Peg would rinse her and soothe her and patch her. But I was ashamed to realize that although I knew the street Peg lived on, I didn't know which house was hers. Who else?

"I've thought of somewhere."

"Where we going?"

"To a safe place."

"Not a doctor!"

"No, I promise."

"Not your house?"

"Not likely."

"Don't touch my bag!"

I jumped back. I'd bumped the bag she had tied around her waist.

"I'm not touching your bag," I said. "But you'll have to walk for us to get anywhere. Breathe deeply, or whatever it takes, because this is a rescue mission." Shaking with cold and hobbling, we left the Way and shuffled into town.

I knew the alleys well enough to worm through Peach Hill without entering the square or using a main street. We moved slowly, but we kept going. How much of her daddy's money did she have in that little bag, I wondered, and how much madder would he be if he knew? What was she planning to do with it? But her breaths were scratchy and it wasn't the time to be asking questions.

There was not a lit window on Crossing Avenue. I hesitated on the pavement, doubting for a moment that I had the right house. Helen sagged against me, and I was afraid she'd faint.

"Come on." I recognized the bamboo window shade. I pulled Helen up the walk and propped her, like a garden ornament, against the porch railing.

"Thank you, Annie," she mumbled. "I need to lie down now."

Nearly too late, I'd remembered something.

"Helen," I whispered. "After you left the other night? At Mr. Poole's house?"

"Uh-huh?"

"Well, I—I—" How to make this sound like a reasonable act? "I pretended I hurt myself, falling from the fence. I pretended my brain went funny so I couldn't tell them anything or give them your name." Helen's one good eye was staring at me intently. "So I haven't been back to school either, since then. Mrs. Newman came to find me and I—I acted loony. So you can't tell her otherwise, okay?"

"You brought me to Mrs. Newman's house?" She wobbled, trying to turn around.

"Helen, you have to get fixed up. It's only for a couple of nights, till we think of something else."

She nodded, closed her eyes and swayed slightly. I knocked on the window that was set into the door. For too long there was no sound. Helen moaned quietly. I knocked again and pressed my ear against the glass. Suddenly, a light went on above our heads—an electric light suspended from the porch ceiling.

A curtain swished to reveal Old Horse's sleepy face. I found myself waving and then pointed at Helen. The curtain twitched again and Mrs. Newman peered out. She looked odd with her hair in braids and no pansied hat on top, her mouth an *Oh!* of bewilderment.

She opened the door at once.

"Heavens!" She stared at Helen in alarm.

"Help," I bleated, in my idiot voice.

Fussing and hushing, Mrs. Newman and her husband maneuvered us into their home. We laid Helen down on the brown-striped sofa and looked at her injuries under the light. Her face was misshapen, livid, swollen on one side. There was dried blood in a trickle next to her ear. One red welt across the back of her knees was deepening to purple.

Tears popped from my eyes without my meaning to cry. Mrs. Newman, kneeling beside Helen, gave her husband a list. "Warm water, vinegar, a clean sponge, ice chips, gauze . . ." He hurried out.

"Who did this?" she asked me, very low.

Helen stirred abruptly. "No one," she mumbled. "I fell down the stairs."

Mrs. Newman looked at me and raised that eyebrow. I shook my head. She knew.

"Have to go." I squeezed Helen's hand and left.

I was running before I noticed, running hard through the dark town, my breath huffing and my heart thudding in my chest. I crossed the square more slowly and crept past the doors of St. Alphonse as the bell rang three times. The wind had died down; the dry leaves lay still on the ground. The windows on Needle Street were black patches under thin moonlight.

I fell asleep without thinking another thought but sprang awake at dawn. It was a moment before I heard the tapping that must have woken me, tiny sharp clicks on the window.

Helen's battered face peered in, paper white with patches of violet and crimson. I motioned her to the kitchen door and drew her in with the first glimmer of day.

"What are you doing here?"

"I left," she whispered. "I'm leaving. I came to get you." She fumbled with the pouch at her waist. "I got money, see? You bring some of yours and we can go together."

"But . . . but . . . what about Mrs. Newman?"

"Aw, Annie, she's a good lady but not for me. You got anything to eat?"

I cut and buttered two thick slices of bread while I tried to think. Just leave? It seemed so simple. Could it be as simple as that? I felt dizzy, felt a whooshing, in my ears; I was trying to hold a thought too big to think.

I'd left places in a hurry before. I could see it all, like in a moving picture. Helen would wait at the doorway listening in case my mother woke up. I would go to the hall closet and pull out a carpetbag. I'd fetch out the sugar sack and take two bundles of money. In my room, I'd pack a change of clothes, some underthings, a sweater and . . . what else? What object did I have that I could not bear to leave behind? Helen would hiss from the kitchen, "Pssst! Hurry!" The photograph of my father was out of reach in my mother's drawer, and it might not even be him. I had no picture of my mother. In the end I'd snatch up my notebook with the little gold pen and toss it into the bag.

Running away . . .

Now I thought of Mama, surprised to find an empty house; pictured her face as she slowly noticed what else was gone; saw her fuming, and then dismayed to realize that her daughter was a coward and a sneak.

What Mama might think shouldn't matter . . . Helen needed me. Or at least, she wanted me enough to ask. Maybe we needed each other. I'd only just found her.

But going with Helen would be running away instead of changing course.

Was that what I wanted? No, I wanted a home, in one place.

Helen watched me.

"You could stay here," I said. A ridiculous suggestion. "I mean, maybe not here, but near here, somewhere safe—"

Her face wrinkled. "So it's no? You have the key but you're staying in the cage?"

"I'm sorry, Helen. I'm . . . I'm not ready to leave yet. But if you run into trouble . . . if you ever need help . . ."

She nodded and blinked. I wrapped the bread in waxed paper and handed it over. Her fingers already gripped the door handle. I felt something rip inside as I watched her shuffle into the alley and away. It was new to me, this feeling, and now I'd had it twice in one week; first when Mama sent Peg away, and here again with Helen. I could only prevent the jagged-edged hole inside me from getting bigger if I stayed very still, if I managed not to breathe or let my head sink down, as it longed to do, between my two sagging shoulders.

No one had ever known me. Peg had loved me, tenderly and loyally, but she'd loved a pretend me. I wouldn't have said that Helen loved me, but everything Helen knew about Annie Grey was a true thing. That had never happened before. Helen had turned me into a friend.

And into a thief. I opened the sugar sack, leaning against the broken-handled bucket in the pantry. I took out two rolls of bills and carried them to my room. Just a precaution, I thought. The scalloped front of my chest of drawers left an inch-high gap above the floor, too narrow for a broom or anything other than knowing fingers; an ideal bank.

I lay on my bed, too sad to sleep, waiting for the day to move along far enough so that I could get up again and start over, telling the truth from now on.

27

In Old English, the word
"silly" meant "blessed."

Eventually, I got hungry and went to the kitchen to make myself the same breakfast I'd given Helen.

I was caught off guard by the sight of Sammy sitting at our kitchen table with a cup of tea and a grin like a present.

"Oh, Annie, dear," said Mama. "Good morning, sleepyhead. We've been waiting." She leaned in close and whispered, "Eyeball," as if she were kissing my cheek. I had forgotten, in the surprise of seeing Sammy, that I was an idiot. Sammy hopped up, tipping half his tea into the saucer in his eagerness. Oh, what was Mama up to now? Hadn't I just resolved *No more*? But here I was, smack in the path of an unavoidable collision!

"We're going out for a walk, darling." Mama spoke carefully to her moronic daughter.

What?

"Why, Mama?" I used a softer version of my dreadful hoot.

"You and me and your little friend, Sam."

Coat, hat, gloves; they dressed me as if I were a child. The nearly sleepless night was catching up with me. My eyelids felt gravelly, my ears full of fog. Sammy took my hand, gently, like a trainer with a performing bear. I couldn't understand how he'd gotten there, or why he was happy, or where they were taking me. And even though I had just decided never to be instructed by Mama again, I went along because of Sammy. Mama had selected good bait.

Closing my eyes while we walked was easier than jiggling my eyeball. From Needle Street to Picker's Lane, onto Main Street and across the square, I glanced down at the curbs, but otherwise I floated, guided by firm hands.

"Here she is!"

"She's here, look, she's coming!"

My eyes flew open at the shouts, and my legs froze to the spot. I jerked my hand from Sammy's and pulled free of Mama's hold. The steps of St. Alphonse were crowded with people, and as I stared, I realized they were mostly people I knew.

It was the hour of morning traffic, with children gathering before school, people pausing on their way to factories and shops and offices.

"*No!*" I shook my head in a frenzy of protest.

"Thank you, Sam," said Mama quickly. "You go on ahead. We'll be there in just another minute. Oh! And pass out the rest of these!" She handed him a sheaf of papers, artfully announcing the morning's event: SEE THE IDIOT RESTORED TO REASON!

"He's a sweet boy," she said vaguely, watching Sammy dash off at her command.

217

"What are you thinking?" I wailed. "I told you *no!* I said I would not participate in a public healing! I am finished, Mama, done! I will not perform another humiliating pantomime. Why can't you hear me?"

"We don't have to make threats or promises about the future," said Mama, too calmly. "All we need right now is one small miracle in front of an excited audience. You can do that much for me, can't you, Annie?"

My voice sighed out like air from a bicycle tire. "No, Mama. I can't do that. I've made a vow not to lie anymore, not to trick people or be a sham."

She laughed, sharply. "Annie, this is not the time. The audience is waiting."

I didn't move.

"Your disloyalty is making me very angry, Annie."

I didn't blink.

She pursed her lips and tried again. "I need you to assist me, darling. . . . If you do not go up those stairs and perform that marvelous twitching seizure of yours, I will be compromised beyond repair. What would become of us then? You're too smart for such silliness, Annie. With that brute of a police officer standing there, you know enough not to put us in danger. So let's just get this over with, shall we? They're becoming impatient."

"I'm sorry, Mama. But I can't. I won't. I'm going to tell them the truth and face whatever consequences come our way."

"I can't go to prison again, Annie. I've never hurt anyone. I do not kill or steal or even cheat, not really. I do my best to comfort people. I give them something to look forward to. Everyone who comes through my door goes back out with a spark of hope."

"Everyone except me, Mama," I whispered. "You never comfort me."

"Oh, Annie."

She reached out to put her hands on my shoulders, but I stepped back. It was too late.

"Annie," she whispered. "Look at all the people waiting. They've come because they believe in me, in both of us. They want the best for you, they want you cured. Can't you give them that?"

I looked toward the crowd to see Sammy waving, urging us on. I knew I had to tell him the truth, but maybe not in front of the whole town. I felt my body relent before my mind had agreed. Mama seized the moment and hurried me along while she could. Sammy, like a little boy with a new wagon, came bounding over to help. I didn't want to look at him. I didn't like holding his hand, because it was under Mama's command.

It seemed that half the population of Peach Hill was gathered outside the old church. They shifted to let us through, but I felt hands patting me, grabbing, rubbing, poking the about-to-be miracle girl.

I squeezed my eyes tight shut to prevent any chance of tears. My toe hit the granite step and I stumbled as Sammy and Mama pulled me upward. I should just collapse, go into a keening fit and be done!

But we'd arrived at the top.

"How I have *prayed*!" cried Mama at once, not waiting to

risk another rebellion. Sammy was still holding my arm, but she waved him off.

"I have not stopped praying." Mama's clear voice rang out like the church bell itself. She stood behind me with her hands on my shoulders. "All night and all day and all night again, since this new affliction befell my dearest girl."

She was doing something with her fingers around my head, not touching but making my scalp itch from the fluttering breeze.

"I am calling on the guardian spirits," said Mama, "who mind us here on the earthly plain. I am pleading for the bright light of my child's smile to be restored to us. Can we all do together what I once did alone?"

There was a ripple of noise, not quite a chorus, but friendly. Mama carried on, beginning to hum now. Sammy waved his arms, urging everyone to join her.

I saw Peg arrive at the back of the crowd, out to do her marketing. She waved and blew me a kiss. Mr. Poole stood by the church railing, his head bowed while he spoke to a man in a battered fedora. I felt a cold lump in my throat. Mr. Poole was the reason I was standing there like an idiot. When he moved, pointing up at Mama and me, I realized that the other fellow had a big camera slung around his neck on a strap.

I glanced back at Mama to see her arms outstretched and her face tipped up to the pale autumn sun, as if receiving a blessing from the Other Side.

Pop! A small flash as the first photograph was taken. "No!" I shouted. *Pop!* "No!"

Mr. Poole had chosen exactly the wrong method of winning us over. Mama looked at me in panic.

"Go, Mama," I said. "Go, now!" She reached out to me, but I was already lunging toward the photographer. People scattered, thinking I was a charging lunatic. *Pop!*

"No pictures!" I yelled, and then tripped, flailing for balance on the stone stairs. The audience gasped, but no one moved quickly enough. I teetered and fell, meeting the ground with a terrible *whack!*

Did I imagine an instant of vibrating silence, or was it real? The pain was real, attacking the same ankle as before and cutting like a cold knife through my forehead. I curled up as tightly as I could and lay on my side, wishing to be anywhere other than there—thinking, this is absolutely the last time, if I live to be ninety-seven, that I huddle on the ground for the benefit of someone else.

"Are you all right, Annie?" Sammy was on his knees next to me.

"Where's Mama?" I said. Did she get away?

"Over there." He pointed in the direction of Picker's Lane and Needle Street. "She's moving pretty fast for an older woman."

"Let me in, that's my girl lying there." Peg pushed her way through, never minding the toes her whopping shoes were treading on. She crouched down, ready to cluck and coo. But one look at her dear, bony nose and springy hair, and I made up my mind.

"I'm all right, Peg! Better than all right!"

Her smile was big enough to have me laughing out loud.

"It worked!" Sammy stood up and shouted to the world. "Annie is healed! The idiot is gone!"

With Sammy and Peg each under one elbow, I was

scooped up from the cobbles, head and ankle howling. The audience cheered. But it wasn't over yet. This was only the first act.

"Wait here," I said to Sammy. "Annie loves Peg," I said to Peg. I limped to the top step and turned to face the crowd.

"Thank you," I said, looking out across the square. Mama's red coat flashed like an ember before she vanished. There was no sign of Mr. Poole or the photographer.

But Sammy was there, and Peg. I focused slowly on the other faces surrounding me. Clusters of schoolchildren and high schoolers; Lexie, Jean and Ruthie, with her mouth wide open; Sally and Delia, who looked more curious than hostile; Frankie Romero, next to his mother. The Peach Hill police department was watching from the sidelines. There were a dozen ladies or more who had spent time in our front room, including Miss Weather and Mildred, who had finally said farewell to her husband at Mr. Poole's party. Mrs. Peers gave me a happy little wave from the front row.

"Thank you for coming here today. I have a confession to make."

"That's inside the church!" somebody called out.

I waited until the laughter faded. "Or perhaps not a confession exactly, but an explanation."

So many of these people had told us secrets, and in return we had told them lies. But they didn't know that. As far as they knew, we'd given hope and sympathy and maybe even wisdom. Would they despair if they were told the truth now? Mildred had been so grateful on Saturday, believing that Edmund's spirit was watching over her. How could I say for certain that he wasn't? Wouldn't it be cruel of me to announce to a grieving woman—to a dozen grieving women—that it had all been a trick?

"My mother has struggled to bring out the best in me," I said, "like most mothers, I guess."

If I destroyed Mama . . . I would rip apart the trust of all these other neighbors and customers.

But I wouldn't tell another lie.

"Mama knew . . . that hiding somewhere was the child she longed for me to be. She did her best to reveal my true nature. Her powers have been put to . . . a remarkable test." Almost over. "In our case, the obstacle was . . . was greater than most. Now that she has released me, my mother will need to recover for an extended time. She will not be accepting clients for . . . for the foreseeable future."

"What about you?" Mrs. Peers called out. "You do a bang-up job yourself."

"I don't think . . . well, that I've inherited the right traits from my mother, whatever it is that inspires her to do this work," I said. "For now, I plan to be an ordinary girl. Thank you." I waved. "My head hurts! I have to sit down. Thank you. Good-bye."

There. Every word I'd said was true, without quite telling the true story.

Most of the kids had hightailed it off even before I'd finished talking; the drama was over, as far as they were concerned. I was just odd Annie Grackle; they were late for school, and Mrs. Newman was circling the crowd.

"Annie." She cupped my face in her gloved hands and inspected me. "That's a nasty bump you've got! You look like a

223

hoodlum! Though not as roughed up as Helen. Annie, your friend Helen has disappeared. You must tell me where she is. She shouldn't be running about by herself. She was terribly hurt."

"She's gone, ma'am. There's nothing we can do anymore."

"Gone? Gone where?"

"Just gone," I said. "She went on the train, but I don't know which way." It hurt to say it out loud.

Mrs. Newman sighed, as if she'd lost something too. "And what about you? That was a brave act just now, Annie Grey. It takes a great deal of courage to choose your own road."

"Mmmm," I said. "I don't think I'll get to school today, Mrs. Newman."

Her eyebrow rose.

"But I'll be there from now on."

"Good girl."

Peg decided it was the right time to interrupt. "Let's get you home, missy, put some ice on that head."

Did Peg realize what I'd been saying up there on the steps? If so, she didn't let on. But I knew that if I arrived on Needle Street with Peg, Mama would be in a poisonous temper. "Peg, Mr. Poole must have hired that photographer without realizing that Mama hates to have her picture taken. She's likely to be hopping mad. I don't think you should come right now."

"She's not going to make your head feel right the way I will," said Peg.

"I know, but also?" I pulled her close, to speak into her

ear, and her curls tickled my nose. "This boy, Sammy, said he'd walk me home. I'd kind of like . . ." I left it dangling.

"Off you go, honey," said Peg, with a sly grin. "But you promise me you'll put an ice pack on your head? And I'm coming over there first thing in the morning, come hell or high water."

Probably both, I thought.

"That," said Sammy, "was the most astounding phenomenon I'll probably witness until I die, of course, and see the gates of Heaven."

"Sammy." I turned to face him. "I wish I—"

"You got healed, didn't you? Before our very eyes."

"Sammy. It wasn't Mama praying or calling on spirits. It wasn't falling down the stairs and giving myself a royal goose egg." I looked into his eyes. "Sammy, here's the truth. My mother and I—"

"Don't say it," said Sammy, shaking his head, closing his dear eyes. "You're going to tell me something I don't want to know."

"Yes, I am." I wished it were dark so we could kiss again. I was sure we were about to say good-bye. How awkward it would be to kiss in daylight! Maybe that was why people closed their eyes to kiss—to create their own night.

Sammy was waiting.

28

A light shining out of the dark in a dream shows that you will finally find the truth in a situation, or the answer you have been seeking.

"Sammy, I'm not who you wish I was. I'm not a psychic and neither is my mother. She doesn't tell fortunes—she tells people what they yearn to hear, what they want their future to hold. And sometimes, because they believe in what she says, they can make it happen for themselves."

"But what about the spirits?" he asked. "She can talk to them, can't she? That part is real, isn't it?"

"No, Sam. That's not true either. No spirits, no trances, no visions, no magic."

"And the healing?" He was nearly whispering. " 'See the Idiot Restored to Reason'?"

"Sammy . . ." This was the hardest part. I would almost rather be an idiot than say it. "I never was an idiot. It was all an act. All of it."

He blinked, the hope chased out of his face. Seconds,

minutes, maybe hours ticked by while Sammy tried to absorb the punches I'd thrown.

"Well, then," he finally said.

"I'm sorry," I said. "I'm so sorry."

"You're still the girl I kissed."

My heart jumped.

"But that's . . . that's all."

I didn't deserve to care so much. I made myself keep looking straight at him.

"Are you leaving Peach Hill?"

"No," I said. "My mother is leaving, but I'm staying on. For now, anyway."

He pushed the dark hair off his forehead. "I suppose I'll see you, then," he said. "I kinda want to think about things."

"Me too," I said. "Let's both think really hard."

"I'd better go to school." He touched my hand, just a tap, really, with his fingertips. "Bye, then."

"Bye."

The walk up Picker's Lane to Needle Street seemed as far and lonely a journey as out to the Way. I stopped at the corner and ducked into a shadowed doorway. Mr. Poole's motorcar was parked outside number sixty-two, with all four doors wide open. Our front door stood ajar as well. I crept closer. I could hear Mama's voice but not her words. She must be somewhere in the back of the apartment. I poked my head into the hall, tempted to slide into the front room, to nestle at my listening post behind the red armchair.

". . . still don't understand why it's so urgent that you leave at once," Mr. Poole was saying.

"A stay in jail is a great educator," said Mama. "And inspires one to move more quickly next time the chance arises."

She'd told him about jail? They were becoming intimate. I'd clearly missed the part where she'd thrown a fit about the photographer, though she still sounded pretty snappy. I retreated to the corner of Picker's Lane. My head ached terribly. I wanted to lie down. I didn't want to talk to Mama with Mr. Poole standing by.

The door banged open. Mr. Poole staggered out, carrying Mama's trunk to the car. Perhaps I wouldn't have a choice. Mama followed with the hatboxes, one of them full of money. Did he know that yet? He brought out the carpetbags and my own suitcase. Where was the sugar sack from the kitchen? Probably stuffed into one of the carpetbags. She couldn't have found the two rolls of money I'd taken after Helen's visit. They were too well hidden in my room.

Mr. Poole came outside and cranked up the car. He got into the driver's seat, and Mama climbed up next to him. I stepped toward the car. Would she really leave without saying good-bye?

"Mama?" I leaned through the window next to her.

Her grin of triumph nearly knocked me over. "I knew you must be watching!" she cried. "I used your suitcase as bait. You see, Gregory? Just as I predicted. She saw us ready to go and here she is!"

My heart cracked in two as I realized that she'd used a trick even now at the end of things. Though I supposed she didn't believe yet that it was the end.

"Gregory says he'll take us as far as Nobel. We can stay

the night there and have a better choice of trains in the morning."

"I'm not going with you, Mama. I'm staying in Peach Hill. I only came to say good-bye. And to wish you well."

"Nonsense," said Mama.

"Not nonsense," I said.

She got down from the car. I reached in behind her and took out my case. She grasped it while I held the handle and we tussled for a moment. I let go and she staggered backward.

"Take it, then," I said. "You can take all of it but me."

Mama dropped the suitcase as if it burned her fingers. I heard Mr. Poole behind me, but she waved at him to shush.

"Let's go inside," she said. We went into the front room. She sat in her own chair, and I sat in the red armchair.

"We've been planning to leave anyway," she said.

"Not me," I said. "I don't see why you'd want to trust Mr. Poole. He's not rich, Mama. He's been conning us all along."

She smiled. "I'll admit that he had me for a day or two," she said, "but I had him first. It was quite a treat to find that there was more to him than I expected. You haven't had a chance to learn this yet, Annie, but you will someday. There's a certain appeal, a relief, even, in finding a companion who cares about who you really are."

I lifted her hand from her lap and turned it over, placing my palm flat against hers before looking carefully at the map of lines.

"I see a long life," I said. "Much of the conflict has been resolved. Adventure and romance await you."

"What will I do without you, Annie?"

I stared at her palm.

"What I want to find out," I said, "is what I'll do without you."

Every sound and every breath of air seemed to leave the rooms with Mama.

The worries I didn't want to face were pounding for attention in that quiet. Where would I live now? The rent was paid until the end of the month. Then what? How long would my stolen money last? Would I like school as much without Mama here to object? How was Helen doing out there in the world alone, if I was afraid right here in Peach Hill?

Oh, my aching head.

Tomorrow, I'd think. I'd find the answers tomorrow.

Peg came early in the morning. She was holding the newspaper, folded back to show Mama's face, uplifted as if in prayer. The headline read: HEALER OR FRAUD?

"You've got some explaining to do, missy," said Peg. "I've been putting two and two and two more together and coming up with half a dozen. Why would you hide all this from me? I'm not happy about looking the fool, not one bit."

"You were never a fool, Peg," I said. "Mama . . ." My voice trailed off.

"Honey?" She patted a salve onto the bump on my forehead. "You know what? You had to get away from that woman. She's got the devil inside her, right into the bones."

"She's my mama, Peg."

"And maybe she even loves you. But she loves herself first, and she's been using you something awful. That's not healthy for a child."

"I wanted to tell you, really I did, but—"

"But nothing. I know," she said. "Get your things. We're going to my house."

My things weren't much: a small pile of clothes, a few books, Mama's silky nightdress, the silver bell that hooked under my séance skirt, and forty twenty-dollar bills.

My little notebook and my gold pen.

One never knows.

Peg's house smelled of vinegar and lemons, as though she'd been scrubbing just for me. She gave me a tour, which took four minutes. A plate of gingersnaps and raspberry jumbles waited on the kitchen table, and Peg soon made a pot of tea. She had knit the tea cozy herself, in the shape of a rabbit.

"Too chilly now to sit outside," she said, "but spring and summer, my little porch is like another room, overlooking the street with the whole world going by. I plant vegetables in April. I hope you like to weed, missy."

"It's nice here," I said. "And I'll get a job after school, Peg. I'll help pay, I promise." If I'd told her I had eight hundred dollars tucked in the lining of my bag, she'd have fainted dead away.

"I start next Monday for Mrs. Tibbet," said Peg. "Laundry and ironing. We'll do all right."

"Yes, we will."

"And I've been seeing a fellow. Just like you said I would. That other policeman? The little one, with the manly voice? Well, it turns out he's quite the dancer and more fun than a circus." She blushed scarlet. "I'm not sure yet, you know, that he's the true love you mentioned, but still. He's a fellow."

"A lucky fellow," I said. "And I like your house, Peg. It feels like a home. But . . ." How to say it? Straight out, I decided. "I don't think I can sleep in the bed where your father died. What if he came to visit?"

"It would serve you right," grumbled Peg. "But I suppose we'd best give away that bed. I can hardly bring myself to fluff the pillows. I know you claim now it's bunkum, but I swear he watches my every move."

"Anything's possible," I said. And I meant it.

(Advertisement from the *Clooney Herald*)

**Readings
by La Bella Katrina
and Master Sebastian
DO NOT LOSE HEART!
Guaranteed Results
This trance medium of Gypsy Blood brings you solutions to
Life's Greatest Mysteries.
If you
HAVE BEEN CROSSED, LOST YOUR LOVE, CANNOT
HOLD MONEY, NEED LUCK, MISLAID PRECIOUS
ITEMS, WISH FOR SOMETHING MORE, DESIRE TO
SPEAK WITH THOSE WHO HAVE PASSED OVER,
La Bella Katrina has the answers you seek.
When your case seems hopeless, there is a remedy for you.
Don't tell her, she'll tell you.
See her in the morning, BE HAPPY AT NIGHT!**

About the Author

Marthe Jocelyn is the author of several award-winning novels and has also written and illustrated picture books. Her most recent novel for Wendy Lamb Books is *Would You*. She lives in Stratford, Ontario.

Visit her on the Web at www.marthejocelyn.com.